MW00953219

Investing in Love

Billionaire Banker Series, Volume 3

Lexy Timms

Published by Dark Shadow Publishing, 2018.

This is a work of fiction. Similarities to real people, places, or events are entirely coincidental.

INVESTING IN LOVE

First edition. October 10, 2018.

Copyright © 2018 Lexy Timms.

Written by Lexy Timms.

Also by Lexy Timms

Investing in Love

Billionaire Holiday Romance Series
Driving Home for Christmas
The Valentine Getaway
Cruising Love

Billionaire in Disguise Series
Facade
Illusion
Charade

Billionaire Secrets Series
The Secret
Freedom
Courage
Trust
Impulse
Billionaire Secrets Box Set Books #1-3

Building Billions
Building Billions - Part 1
Building Billions - Part 2
Building Billions - Part 3

Conquering Warrior Series
Ruthless

Diamond in the Rough Anthology
Billionaire Rock
Billionaire Rock - part 2

Dominating PA Series
Her Personal Assistant - Part 1
Her Personal Assistant Box Set

Fake Billionaire Series
Faking It
Temporary CEO
Caught in the Act
Never Tell A Lie
Fake Christmas

Firehouse Romance Series
Caught in Flames
Burning With Desire
Craving the Heat
Firehouse Romance Complete Collection

For His Pleasure
Elizabeth
Georgia
Madison

Fortune Riders MC Series
Billionaire Biker
Billionaire Ransom
Billionaire Misery

Fragile Series
Fragile Touch
Fragile Kiss
Fragile Love

Hades' Spawn Motorcycle Club
One You Can't Forget
One That Got Away
One That Came Back
One You Never Leave
One Christmas Night
Hades' Spawn MC Complete Series

Hard Rocked Series

Rhyme
Harmony

Heart of Stone Series
The Protector
The Guardian
The Warrior

Heart of the Battle Series
Celtic Viking
Celtic Rune
Celtic Mann
Heart of the Battle Series Box Set

Heistdom Series
Master Thief
Goldmine
Diamond Heist
Smile For Me

Just About Series
About Love
About Truth
About Forever

Justice Series
Seeking Justice
Finding Justice
Chasing Justice
Pursuing Justice
Justice - Complete Series

Love You Series
Love Life
Need Love
My Love

Managing the Bosses Series
The Boss
The Boss Too
Who's the Boss Now
Love the Boss
I Do the Boss
Wife to the Boss
Employed by the Boss
Brother to the Boss
Senior Advisor to the Boss
Forever the Boss
Christmas With the Boss
Gift for the Boss - Novella 3.5

Model Mayhem Series
Shameless
Modesty
Imperfection

Moment in Time
Highlander's Bride
Victorian Bride
Modern Day Bride
A Royal Bride
Forever the Bride

Outside the Octagon
Submit

Protecting Diana Series
Her Bodyguard
Her Defender
Her Champion
Her Protector
Her Forever

Protecting Layla Series
His Mission

Battle Lines

The Brush Of Love Series
Every Night
Every Day
Every Time
Every Way
Every Touch

The Debt
The Debt: Part 1 - Damn Horse
The Debt: Complete Collection

The University of Gatica Series
The Recruiting Trip
Faster
Higher
Stronger
Dominate
No Rush
University of Gatica - The Complete Series

T.N.T. Series
Troubled Nate Thomas - Part 1
Troubled Nate Thomas - Part 2
Troubled Nate Thomas - Part 3

Worth Billions
Worth Every Cent
Worth More Than Money

You & Me - A Bad Boy Romance
Just Me
Touch Me

Standalone
Wash
Loving Charity
Summer Lovin'
Love & College
Billionaire Heart
First Love
Frisky and Fun Romance Box Collection
Managing the Bosses Box Set #1-3

Watch for more at www.lexytimms.com.

Investing
IN LOVE
USA TODAY BESTSELLING AUTHOR
LEXY TIMMS

Copyright 2018

All rights reserved.
Investing in Love
Billionaire Banker Series #3
Copyright 2018 by Lexy Timms
Cover by: Book Cover by Design[1]

---

1. http://bookcoverbydesign.co.uk/

Billionaire Banker Series

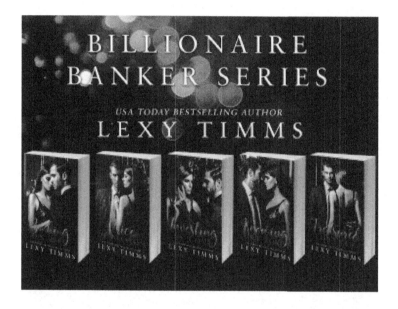

Book 1 – Banking on Him
Book 2 – Price of Passion
Book 3 – Investing in Love
Book 4 – Knowing Your Worth
Book 5 – Treasured Forever

Find Lexy Timms:

LEXY TIMMS NEWSLETTER:
http://eepurl.com/9i0vD
Lexy Timms Facebook Page:
https://www.facebook.com/SavingForever
Lexy Timms Website:
http://www.lexytimms.com

Want to read more...
For **FREE**?
Sign up for Lexy Timms' newsletter
And she'll send you updates on new releases, ARC copies of books
and a whole lotta fun!
Sign up for news and updates!
http://eepurl.com/9i0vD

Investing in Love Blurb

BY USA TODAY BESTSELLING Author, Lexy Timms.

Love like you're never counting the cost.

Kirk Sterling hasn't seen Bethany Walker since the day he dumped her. He broke up with her to protect her from his powerful family, but he hasn't gotten over her. When Bethany shows up, desperate for his help, Kirk agrees, ready to resist her seductive charm.

After her breakup with Kirk, Bethany Walker has kept her distance, working hard to move on from her heartache. But she discovers that her estranged father is in danger, and Kirk is the only man she can turn to for help. Seeing Kirk again threatens to reignite the feud between their families; worst of all, it endangers her battered heart.

Working together is the toughest challenge either of them has faced. As they uncover the secrets of the past and get closer to the shocking truth, danger lurks around every corner. Will Kirk and Bethany rekindle their relationship, or will the war between their families consume them both?

Chapter 1

The Sterling Investment Tower loomed ominously over her, casting a dark shadow over the people below it. Bethany Walker shivered despite the warmth of the day. Her heart was in her throat. Walking back into Sterling Investment Bank was something she had vowed never to do. Now she was about to break that promise. Break it and walk into the place that had caused so much destruction.

Leveling her shoulders, she forced herself to march in past the glass doors. She stopped at one of the desks up front and plastered a wide, phony smile on her face.

The secretary at the front desk returned her smile and greeted her warmly.

"Hi, my name is Bethany Walker. I'm here to see Mr. Sterling," Bethany said.

"Which Mr. Sterling?" the secretary asked.

Of course. She was going to have to be more specific. To Bethany's knowledge, there were at least five Mr. Sterlings. The one Sterling she had to immediately see was the only one with the power to crush her heart into dust. Like he had so many weeks ago.

Her mouth went dry. This poor secretary had no clue about all the fretful thoughts running through her head right now, and it wouldn't be fair to be anything other than courteous. She cleared her throat. "Kirk. Kirk Sterling."

"Just a moment please." The secretary reached for the phone on her desk. "Is he expecting you this morning?"

"No." Bethany felt her throat clog with emotion as she remembered the way Kirk had turned his back on her. "He isn't."

The secretary's inviting demeanor turned cold as she gave a disapproving frown. "I'm sorry, but we have a strict policy at Sterling Investment Bank. All meetings with Mr. Sterling must be scheduled."

"He knows me," she blurted out. "Kirk and I are..." Her heart squeezed so painfully against her ribs that she had to pause. What were she and Kirk to each other? Enemies? Acquaintances? Former lovers? Maybe they were all those things. Maybe they were nothing. "We've worked together in the past," she said finally.

"Perhaps you can leave a message with me so that I can deliver it to him," the secretary said. "I assure you that I'll deliver the message personally."

No. This was far too important to leave as a message with a stranger. The matter was too sensitive to let just anyone in on it. But if she didn't give the secretary something, she'd no doubt be stonewalled and prevented from seeing Kirk.

"This is a private matter," Bethany murmured. "One that might affect the bank's reputation."

"Oh." The secretary's eyes narrowed in suspicion. "You're not a reporter, are you?"

"No. I'm definitely not," she replied, her voice wavering as her nerves got the better of her. "Could you contact him and let him know I'm here? This is an emergency and I'm sure he'll want to see me." She wasn't sure of that at all, of course. After Kirk had gotten her out of jail and dropped her off at her apartment, she hadn't seen him. At least, not up close. There had been a story about a glitzy fundraiser on the local news and she had spotted him on TV. Other than that, she hadn't laid eyes on Kirk in weeks.

"Perhaps it's best if you call Mr. Sterling and schedule a meeting yourself. Since you're so close to him, you must have his number." The secretary sized her up warily, no doubt trying to figure out the nature of the relationship between them. From the way her lips thinned in disapproval, it was clear that the secretary thought Bethany was some kind of scorned lover. Which she was. In a way. She had been jilted. But she would never come here to trouble Kirk's peace.

Even though she had taken on her mother's last name, she was also a Livingston. And as a Livingston she had way too much dignity to play the part of the stalker ex, no matter how devastated she was about Kirk dumping her.

"I've left voice messages on his phone," Bethany lied. There was no use telling the secretary that Kirk probably wouldn't have taken her calls even if she had made them. Her only contact with Kirk was through the lawyer he had paid to handle her arrest several weeks ago. The lawyer had instructed her to give his law office a call if she was in any further legal trouble, but she wasn't in that kind of trouble. At least, not at the moment.

"Well, I can't promise anything, but I'll call him. Even so, I doubt he'll want to be interrupted since he's very busy this week." The secretary tapped her fingers on the keypad and paused as the call went through. "This is the front desk. Is Mr. Sterling available? Yes, I'll hold for transfer."

Bethany chewed her lower lip as she waited through the most excruciating sixty seconds of her life.

"Mr. Sterling? Yes, this is the front desk. There's a Bethany Walker here to see you." The secretary went silent for a beat and then nodded. "She says it's an emergency of a sensitive nature. Certainly, sir. Goodbye."

The secretary hung up. "Mr. Sterling will see you in his office. Do you know where it is?"

Bethany nodded. Though she hadn't visited SIB headquarters often when her father had been the one running the bank, she knew the layout of the building well enough. Plus, she had been to Kirk's office before. They had even fooled around in his office on one occasion. Heat rose in her cheeks at the memory of how intimate they had gotten then. "Yes, I can find my way there."

Barely able to believe her luck, she quickly said goodbye to the secretary and dashed to the elevator. She had to get to Kirk's office before he had changed his mind or ordered security to throw her out. As desperately as she needed to see him, she hadn't thought it would be this easy to get him to meet with her.

When she exited the elevator Bethany headed down the hallway, stopping at his assistant's desk outside his office.

His assistant glanced up from her laptop. "Bethany, right?"

She nodded. "Yes."

"You can head straight inside," the assistant said with a wave of her hand.

Clutching the strap of her handbag for strength, Bethany took a deep sigh and headed to Kirk's office door. She put her hand on the doorknob for a second to momentarily gather her courage. Then she straightened her spine and walked inside.

———◦●◦———

KIRK WAS STANDING IN front of the office windows, his hands jammed inside his pockets as he looked down at the street below.

"You're here," he said without turning around to face her.

The way he spoke so matter-of-factly made her wonder if he had been expecting her. But how could that be? She hadn't known she'd be dropping by his office until last night.

Her stomach tightened as her gaze landed on him.

His bulky frame seemed to take over the expansive office, making everything seem small compared to him. Though she couldn't see the expression on his face, he still had a commanding presence. He was tall, with broad shoulders, radiating an air of power underneath that expensive, elegant suit he was wearing.

"Yes. I am." It was the only thing she could think to say under the circumstances.

When he turned around to look at her, she had to force herself to breathe. She had almost forgotten just how handsome he was. With dark hair that fell over hypnotizing green eyes, he had the looks of a movie star. The healthy tan and chiseled jaw only added to his good looks.

"What brings you here?" It wasn't a question. There was no curiosity here. None of the careful concern he had showered on her when they had reunited after he had forgiven all her lies. This was a demand. The demand of the vice president of one of the most important financial institutions in the world. There was impatience in his tone. Dismissal in his eyes.

It broke her already-shattered heart all over again. Clearly, Kirk hadn't missed her as much as she had missed him. Worse, it was more likely that he hadn't even missed her at all.

She had cried her eyes out after he had abruptly dumped her. Cried for days. Then, after the crying had stopped, she had walked around in a bewildered daze. The pain of him abandoning her had been so great that her body had gone into a sort of numb, protective shock. Seeing him now was like having a bucket of ice water thrown on her. The numb shock was now being replaced by biting, chilling pain.

"I need your help." Again. For her entire adult life she had been forced to fend for herself. Forced to take care of herself because nobody else would. But then she had met Kirk and had found herself leaning on him. Even more surprising, for most of the time she had known him he had wanted her to lean on him. He'd welcomed it. Like a knight in shining armor who had come to shoulder her burdens. Until he had dropped her off at her apartment and told her never to contact him.

That was a command she had intended to follow to the letter. The past twelve hours had changed everything, however.

"With what?"

Heart thudding in her chest she took several steps toward him, undaunted by the indifference in his eyes. "I'm still investigating the embezzlement."

He frowned. "Still trying to clear your father's name, you mean."

She bristled at the judgment in his tone. Though the things she had recently learned were testing her resolve, she still believed in her father's innocence. Things with her father were more strained than they had ever been, but she had to believe in him.

Ten years ago, her father had been put in prison for financial fraud and embezzlement. As the wealthy president of the Livingston Bank, her father had overseen staggering amounts of money throughout his career. But she had always benefited from his own, personal wealth that he inherited from his parents. Wealth that he had grown with his work as the head of the Livingston Bank. Which meant that he couldn't possibly have had a motive to defraud people out of their hard-earned wealth. The charge had never made sense to her. Not that the media or the justice system had cared. Foregoing a trial that could have proven his innocence, her poor father had taken a plea deal and spent a decade in prison.

"Yes. I believe in my father. Even if nobody else does," she said with a defiant lift of her chin. She wasn't going to let on that his words were getting to her. How could she tell him that doubts about her father had started to creep in?

A decade without her father had been a nightmare. A nightmare made worse by the fact that Kirk's parents had been responsible for her father's arrest. The Sterlings and the Livingstons had been at odds even before her father's fall, and her secret relationship with Kirk had only made tensions flare. They had been enemies, on opposing sides in a war the families had waged for years. At first, she had been totally loyal to her father. So loyal that she had plotted to bring Kirk down with the rest of his family. That plan had changed when she started to fall for Kirk. As she got to know him, she developed deep feelings for him.

Feelings she couldn't ignore no matter how hard she tried. They had been forced to meet in secret because of the feud, but when their families discovered the truth Kirk had abruptly and painfully ended things between them to keep her safe from his parents' wrath.

"Does your father believe in you?" Kirk asked. "Has he forgiven you for... what happened between us?"

Her lower lip trembled. "No. He hasn't." They weren't even on speaking terms. Soon after Kirk ended things, her father moved out of her apartment. Though her father was now living with her brother, she hadn't seen either of them since the move. Worse, even though her brother occasionally talked to her on the phone, her father hadn't called or sent a message. It was like she had been rendered invisible. Her father had disowned her, and it looked like he was sticking to that decision despite her breakup with Kirk.

"Lloyd Livingston always was a fool," he bit out.

"It doesn't matter. I didn't come here to get you to approve of my father."

"What did you come for, then?" he asked.

She took a deep breath. Her legs were shaking as anxiety flooded her. It was now or never. "I've come to request SIB's financial records." Bethany narrowed her eyes to let him know that she meant business. "Going back twenty years."

Chapter 2

I t was an outrageous request. If it had come from anybody else, it would be insulting. Laughable.

Kirk's eyes swept over her. From the deathly serious look on her face, this was no laughing matter for her. Bethany meant every word.

"I'm sorry, but I'm declining your request." His jaw tightened.

"You can't."

He forced back a derisive laugh. Only a Livingston could be this arrogant. This audacious. Kirk hated to admit it, but he still found Bethany's boldness intriguing. There was something thrilling about the way she reached for what she wanted, even if it was forbidden. That was why her presence in his office was so dangerous. Her unexpected arrival this morning had thrown him off balance. Made him lose his head long enough to invite her into his office. He should have known that inviting her was really just inviting trouble.

"I can." He looked down his nose at her, keeping his face as expressionless as possible. Letting her see the effect she had on him would only make the trouble worse. Seeing her again after all this time made his heart pound so hard that he had to fight to catch his breath.

Her blond hair was pulled back in a tight bun, revealing the delectable flesh of her slender neck. Swallowing hard, Kirk allowed himself to indulge in taking her in. His gaze swept up her neck to her kissable, bee-stung lips. He had tasted that mouth of hers more than once, and now all he wanted to do was taste it again. Taste it and let his teeth drag across the fullness of her lower lip.

"Why won't you let me see the records?" she demanded, dragging him from his thoughts before they got even more carnal and inappropriate. Pure defiance flashed in her eyes.

The nerve of her to push back on him. To make demands, when he was the one with the power and she was the one at his mercy. Yet here she was, asking an outrageous favor. Frustration and admiration struck him in equal measure. She really was magnificent.

A fire blazed in her eyes as she took a step towards him. She put a hand on her hip. "Well? Answer me."

If he had any sense at all, he'd toss her out. For both their sakes. Every moment he spent with Bethany put her at risk of ending up in jail. His mother would gladly send her stooges on the local police force after Bethany. Yet he was too fascinated by her sudden presence to throw her out of here. "Because there isn't a company on earth that would hand over that kind of information. It's a ridiculous request. I'm sure you know that."

She hesitated, her face faltering as her serious expression vanished. "It is ridiculous." Her eyes lowered, and for the first time he noticed that she was shaking like a leaf.

All that defiance had taken incredible strength. Which meant the situation she was in had to be dire. That sent fear through his gut. If Bethany was in trouble he'd never be able to send her away. His need to protect her wasn't even conscious anymore. It was pure instinct now. "Something's wrong. What is it?"

Bethany took several halting steps towards him until she was standing so close he caught the scent of her sinful perfume. "I found out something last night that might change everything."

"Tell me," he commanded.

"I've been investigating the embezzlement," she murmured. "I even had my brother's ex-girlfriend look into it. She's a tech whiz, so getting her to agree to help was a big deal. Anyway, she found an internal memo that my father sent while he was still president of the Livingston Bank."

"He sent the memo before my parents took the bank from him." He narrowed his eyes. "If your tech whiz got access to a memo like that, she had to have gotten her way onto one of SIB's servers. That's hacking."

Bethany met his gaze and threw her shoulders back, standing a little straighter. "What are you going to do, call the cops on us?"

"I should."

She gasped. "You wouldn't dare."

"You don't know what I would do," he retorted.

"I know you well enough to know you'd never do that," she shot back.

"Time has passed since the last time you saw me," he reminded her. "You don't know what I'm capable of now."

"It hasn't been that long," she said quietly.

But it had been. At least, it had felt that way to him. Mere weeks might have passed, but without Bethany it had felt like eternity. Instead of drowning himself in booze, he had thrown himself into his work in a desperate attempt to get over her. He had worked like crazy for weeks to get his mind off her and to regain his father's trust. His father had been furious when he learned about Kirk's secret liaisons with Bethany. So furious that the old man had threatened to cut Kirk out of succeeding as SIB's president. For Kirk, the thought of his brother inheriting the coveted president position was too much to take. Losing Bethany had been hell. Losing the bank to his brother would have been adding insult to injury.

The only thing that had stopped his father's rage was a promise to spend every waking moment devoted to the bank and nothing else. Handing over bank records to a Livingston would shred Kirk's promise. Not only would he lose the chance to become bank president, he'd lose his VP position and his family. Being with Bethany had almost ripped his family apart. The only thing that had prevented that from happening was his promise to turn his back on a relationship with her.

Worse, his father was still hell-bent on Kirk projecting stability to attract old-money investors to the bank. That meant Kirk was expected to learn to fit in with the old families he didn't trust, and was expected to find a stable relationship. After Bethany, he couldn't so much as look at another woman. Just thinking about dating anyone but her filled him with cold dread. While he could distract his father by being devoting himself to work again, he'd soon be expected to find a girlfriend that the old families would approve of. The thought was like a noose around his neck. Bethany's presence only made that noose feel even tighter.

"I couldn't give you those records even if I wanted to," he finally said. "I'm on thin ice as it is with my father."

"Your parents have forgiven you for being with me?"

"Barely. One more wrong move and they'll leave my brother in charge of the bank," he said. "Answering to him isn't something I'm going to do."

"You answer to your father," she pointed out.

"That's different. You'd take orders from your own father, but not your brother." Just thinking about Bethany's hot-head of a brother made Kirk angry. Her brother had been the one to tell her father about their relationship.

"You have a point." She sighed. "I still need to see the bank's records."

"After your friend breached our cyber-security?" He narrowed his eyes. "I really should call the police."

"The memo that my friend found was on one of my father's old personal servers. It isn't connected to the bank's current accounts," she said. "So, she didn't breach the bank's security in any major way."

He frowned. "I thought the police would have gotten their hands on that server."

"My father took a plea deal. There wasn't any need for the police to gather a mountain of evidence since there wasn't a trial. Besides, the government was way more focused on stuff connected to the bank." She tilted her head to scrutinize him. "Haven't you been doing your own investigation into the embezzlement? You must know about that server."

"I stopped the investigation after I..." *After I abandoned you.* He cringed at the voice inside his head that still judged him for how he had ended things between them. Maybe he had been harsh, but it was the only way to make sure Bethany didn't try to come back to him. Besides, cutting her out of his life had worked. Until now.

"After we broke up," she said diplomatically.

After he broke things off with her, he had closed his investigation into her father's crimes. Looking into her father reminded him too much of her. The pain of it had been too much. Shutting it down was the only way he had been able to move forward.

"Well, *I* didn't stop investigating," she continued. "Getting the truth is the only way to make peace between our families."

He scoffed. "You still believe peace between our families is possible?"

"I do."

Bethany had often been more optimistic than he was, despite how cruel life had been to her.

"What was in the memo?" he asked. "What could be so bad that you need to go through twenty years of bank records?"

She glanced down, obviously too distressed to keep her gaze on him. Her shoulders started to shake again and she wrapped her arms around herself. Whatever she had discovered was clearly taking a serious toll on her.

The urge to comfort her forced him to lift his hands, but he thought better of it and lowered them. Touching her would stir something in him that didn't need to be stirred. He had closed the door on them. Closed it and then barred it shut. Nothing was going to pry it open.

"My father had contacted a bankruptcy lawyer months before his arrest," she said.

"What?" he asked, in complete shock. "That means—"

"It means that either my father was seriously in debt or the Livingston Bank was," she said, interrupting him. "It means that he might have had a motive to steal all that money."

It was impossible to say which was worse. If Lloyd Livingston's bankruptcy had been personal, the consequences would have been enormous. Squandering his inherited wealth would have meant his family ending up in the poorhouse. His reputation as a financial genius would have been destroyed and he would probably have been forced to step down from his position as bank president. Calling that a humiliation would have been an understatement.

On the other hand, if Livingston had run the bank into the ground, a crisis of that magnitude would have gone beyond the personal and roiled financial markets. It was the kind of thing that sent stocks crashing. Life savings could disappear in the blink of an eye. Insurance might cover some of the damages, but shareholders would have been protected long before actual clients of the bank.

Either way, a bankruptcy in a personal or professional capacity would have been disastrous. No wonder Livingston had embezzled all that money. He had probably been trying to cover his massive mistake or prop up his financial empire before it collapsed.

He shook his head in disbelief. "You found a motive, and yet you still believe your father is innocent?"

"Yes." Her voice was faint. As if she couldn't muster enough strength to speak above a whisper.

"Why? How can you still believe in him?"

"Because I have to," she cried. "Believing in my father is all I have left."

"That's not true. You're working on looking for a location for your store. I know for a fact that Jane is still helping you set everything up."

Surprise made her eyes widen. "How do you know that?"

Damn it, he'd said too much. Given away a detail that he shouldn't have. Trying to appear as casual as possible, he shrugged. "The bank is still handling Jane Tanner's money, so I've been updated on her investment into your store."

He stopped for a moment, seeing disbelief crease her brow. Clearly she wasn't buying his explanation. Kirk sighed heavily. "I kept tabs on you. After things ended. I've been updated on Jane's investment into your store since that ended up causing you a lot of trouble."

"You've been keeping tabs on me?"

He groaned inwardly and nodded. He'd said too much already. Thanks to his mother's vengeful paranoia, she'd had Bethany arrested on bogus charges. The charges hadn't stuck, but he had made sure to keep an eye on her store's financial issues just in case his mother tried to use it against her again.

"Why?"

After a long pause, he turned away from her to walk back to the window. Staring out at the city below often cleared his head. Put everything into perspective. But with Bethany here in his office, her presence seemed to dim everything around him. Having her here again made the rest of the world so small. So inconsequential.

He couldn't think straight around her. The healthy distance he had fought to maintain all these weeks meant nothing now. Kirk had to wrench back control. "Because I'm responsible for what happens to you. It's my fault my mother came after you, and keeping an eye on things is the right thing to do."

That was all he could tell her. All the tension between them could allow. Telling Bethany that he was having an impossible time getting over her was far too dangerous.

"Well, I'm responsible for looking out for *my* family," she said firmly. "I have to believe in my dad. If I don't, what else will I have to hold on to? My family has been torn apart. I have to bring us all back together. Somehow."

"You have your store to hold on to," he reminded her. "Your dreams."

He heard a soft rustle behind him, the sign that she was heading towards him. When she stopped at his side to stare out the window, neither of them said anything for several long moments. The tension in the air seemed to grow. Expand until the silence was nearly unbearable. Though he hadn't known her for long, Kirk had often felt like he had known Bethany for years. She had been easy to talk to. So charming. So effervescent. It was easy for people who had grown up upper class to appear pretentious. Not her. Even when she talked about travelling across Europe, or Italian wine, she was always so down-to-earth about it all. Always so ready to share her knowledge with him rather than use it as a way to appear superior.

But that was gone. Had breaking up with her hurt her so much that they couldn't even speak freely now? He didn't blame her if she was guarded around him now. Didn't blame her, but couldn't ignore the pain that it caused him.

She turned to look at him. "My dreams are nothing without the people I care about."

When he met her gaze she didn't turn away. Didn't retreat. Bethany kept her blue eyes on him, her gaze so steady he wondered if he was one of the people she cared about.

No. He shook that thought away. It didn't matter if she cared about him. No more than it mattered if she didn't. "Bethany, I hope you understand that it's over between us." As harsh as it was to say, he had to make that clear.

Her eyes darkened with something. Disappointment? Indignation? "If it's over then you should have no problem sharing the bank records with me," she said. "There's no danger of anything happening between us, if that's what you're afraid of. Plus, I know that your mother is in Europe at the moment. She won't be in town to hurt me while I go over the records."

Kirk swallowed a smile. Knowing that she was still interested in his life gave him some satisfaction, though that wasn't going to change anything. "You've been keeping tabs on me as well."

"I've been keeping tabs on your mother." She narrowed her eyes. "Since she's out of the country, now is the safest time to hand over those records. We might not get another chance like this for months."

"Giving you those files is a major breach in our security. Not only is it unethical, but the bank could sue you for looking at confidential files. And that's if my father decided to be merciful. If he found out, pressing charges against you wouldn't be unreasonable. You know how traumatic an arrest is." Watching her get hauled out of his mansion by the police had devastated him like nothing else ever had. The sheer terror in her eyes had haunted him for weeks.

"Please, Kirk." A hopelessness he'd never known was possible for her flickered across her face. "I wouldn't have come to ask this favor if it wasn't life or death."

"Life or death?" His eyebrows shot up. "It can't be that serious—"

"It is. I know my father has reached out to some of the ex-cons he was friends with in prison, and I think he's planning something with them. Something to get back at your parents for what they did to him. These men aren't embezzlers. They're hardened criminals. Armed robbers, drug lords, mob enforcers." She shuddered. "I think he handled their accounts while he was in prison. These men are dangerous, and I don't think my dad understands how in over his head he is."

He shook his head, shocked that her father seemed to be committed to going all in with criminals. The man was getting a second chance with his freedom but he seemed to want to squander it on revenge. On shutting his only daughter out of his life. What kind of fool would choose anything over Bethany?

That notion knocked the wind right out of him. *He* was the kind of fool who would do that. Kirk had tossed her aside and left her to fend for herself. It didn't matter that he had made sure she always had a lawyer at her disposal if she ended up in legal trouble again. She had been on her own without a man to protect her. Again.

"Kirk? You do realize this means my father might be plotting something dangerous for you and your family, don't you?" she continued. "I know I don't have the right to ask for a favor, but this is also a warning. A warning and a reminder that my father hasn't given up on getting revenge. Which means you and your parents are in danger."

"How would giving you the bank records help anything?" he demanded.

"It might help us figure out the truth. If my father is guilty then maybe he can be reasoned with. He might listen if he realizes he can't hide from the truth anymore. It could put a stop to the feud once and for all if he's forced to face what he's done."

"But you believe he's innocent," Kirk said, unable to hide the bitterness in his tone.

"If he's innocent, then that actually makes things harder." She heaved out a sigh and rubbed her eyes. "But if we prove his innocence and publicly clear his name, maybe he can start to heal."

"Or that might just make him angrier," he said. "Imagine spending ten years in prison for a crime you didn't commit."

"Yes. Imagine," she said softly. "If he *is* innocent, he doesn't have to imagine it."

Her words cut through him like a knife. Lloyd Livingston didn't deserve to have a daughter like Bethany. The fool had disowned her, yet here she was. In the office of her enemy. Still fighting for her father. Kirk had never seen this kind of loyalty and devotion in his life. It stunned him.

Getting to the truth about the embezzlement could backfire on them and actually intensify this feud between the Livingstons and the Sterlings. But their only chance to stop the feud was to get the truth out. Let the chips fall and proceed from there. Without the truth, this war would never end. With it, there was at least a slim chance to end the suffering.

"I can't give you twenty years of records," he said firmly. Her face fell, and as she opened her mouth to counter him his hands went up to quiet her. "The best I can do is access five years of records. Starting five years before your father's arrest and leading up until he was forced out as bank president. That way we won't be getting caught up with records under my parents' management."

"You're trying to protect their secrets," she said with a frown.

"It's my final offer." He gave her a hard stare. "You're not going to go snooping through my parents' business activities, Bethany."

She chewed her lower lip and nodded. "Okay. When will you be able to hand the records over to me?"

"I won't be handing over anything to you. The records will never leave my possession. You can look at them, but I sure as hell won't be handing them over to you," he said, making sure she heard the warning in his tone. "Do we have a deal?"

Chapter 3

"Do I really have a choice?" she asked, unwilling to hide the apprehension that laced every word.

Merely looking at the bank's records meant that she would have to spend more time with Kirk. She hadn't anticipated that she would have to spend time with him to get access to the records. Honestly, she'd had doubts that Kirk would have even agreed to see her. She hadn't planned this far ahead.

The expression on his handsome face darkened. Turned more dangerous. "Beggars can't be choosers."

Gone was all the willingness to help her. He had kept tabs on her, but it was obviously out of obligation. Whatever care he had for her must have long disappeared by now. His mother's threats had hardened his heart. Turned it to stone and made him so much colder now. So much harsher.

It was like they were strangers to each other. Only this wasn't like the day they met, when they had shared so much of themselves. She had lied to him when she first met him, and kept so much of herself hidden, but Kirk hadn't been like that at all. During their first encounter he had been so open. So ready to help her. Not this time.

"When can I see the records?" she asked.

"Not now," he answered. "You'll only be able to look at hard copies, but I refuse to give you digital files. I can't have this information leaking out."

Her heart squeezed in pain. Kirk didn't trust her. While he had every reason not to, and was only trying to protect the bank, it still hurt her to know it. "Should we schedule a day for me to come back to your office?"

He shook his head. "We can't meet here. It's too big a risk and we can't chance being caught."

"So, where do we meet?" she asked. "Your place?"

"I don't know if my mother's private investigator is still trailing you," he pointed out. "If you show up to my house suddenly that would look suspicious."

"It would, but what choice do we have?" she asked. "I haven't caught anybody following me in weeks, so I doubt your mother is still having her PI follow me around."

"My mother has her ways," he muttered.

"Well, she's out of the country so that might give us the upper hand," she reminded him.

"Okay. Give me time to get the records together," he said. "I'll message you in a few days when everything is ready and you can come down to my place."

Butterflies fluttered in her stomach at the thought of being alone with him in his mansion again. They'd shared their first kiss there. Gotten to know each other on his property. Memories of having incredible sex in his bedroom made her face blaze with heat.

Even though she had originally resented him for having such an opulent home because of her father's suffering, she had grown attached to the place. The privacy had allowed her to see the kind, caring, generous side of him. The side he often hid while he ruthlessly advanced his family's business interests.

"I guess it's settled then," she said.

He gave a curt nod. "See you in a few days."

His abrupt dismissal of her made her ache all over. It was like every part of her was being ripped apart all over again and she had no way to make it stop. Desperate to hold on to her dignity, she breathlessly said, "Thank you for your help. I'll get out of your way now." She turned away from him and rushed out of his office. It wasn't until she stepped out of the bank that she even realized tears were welling in her eyes.

BETHANY GOT A MESSAGE from Kirk several days later and drove to his seaside mansion. Before she had gotten into her car she had agonized over what to wear. Putting on one of her few well-tailored designs might make it look like she was trying too hard to impress a man who clearly didn't want her. Wearing her worn, slightly shabby clothes would give the wrong impression and make it look like she hadn't put much thought into her appearance. Eventually she had settled on a nice blouse, jeans, and some stylish sandals she had bought herself recently. With Jane Tanner's financial help with her store, she could afford a few nice things now. Too bad she had no family to share her newfound success with.

When she finally arrived at Kirk's mansion, the guards at the ornate front gate let her in and she drove up the long driveway. The sun was already setting and the lights on the property were lit, giving the place a warm, inviting glow. She parked her car in the garage like Kirk had instructed and made her way to the front entrance.

Kirk's rather dour-looking butler, Rathbone, answered the door and led her to the living room. Kirk was sitting on one of the luxurious sofas, still dressed in the black business suit he must have worn to work. With her keen sense of fashion, she knew immediately that the designer suit was well tailored and probably British-made. It fit him perfectly. Not that he had ever needed anything to enhance his rugged masculinity.

As much as she was studying him, Kirk's attention was focused on the stack of papers in his hands.

Once Rathbone announced her, the butler spun on his heel and vanished.

Kirk's gaze flickered up to her face, his green eyes piercing through her. Pinning her in place. Her insides turned to jelly under his harsh scrutiny. With his eyes locked on hers she felt like prey. Because she was at the mercy of his whims. All he had to do was deny her request and she would be done for. If Kirk didn't stick to his promise to help her, there would be no chance of clearing her father's name. No chance to bring her family back together. The only path to ending this feud and saving both their families was to get to the truth. But getting that depended on Kirk. A man who would rather be doing anything else in this moment than entertaining her.

His gaze turned into a momentary scowl, but he quickly gestured to the sofa across from him.

There were so many files and overstuffed folders that she had to take some off the sofa to find a space to sit. Paperwork was scattered across the living room chairs and tables, turning the usually elegant room into a cluttered mess.

As she sat amidst the clutter, she didn't know how to break the ice between them. All she could muster was a mumbled, "Thanks for doing this."

"Save your thanks for when we find something useful," he said bluntly. "Grab a folder and start looking."

She glanced around, too overwhelmed to know where to start. "There are so many files here."

"And this is just five years' worth," he said. "Imagine if this was the twenty years you requested."

"How did you get this out without anyone seeing you?" she asked.

He arched an eyebrow. "There was no way I'd be able to smuggle all this out without being seen. I just made a big show of needing the archive room cleaned and volunteered to take these files home for safe keeping."

Guilt stabbed through her painfully. None of this was his fault, and yet she had dragged him into this mess. The only thing that kept her from ending this right now was knowing that her father was up to something dangerous. Now that her dad was plotting something with his prison buddies, she knew it was only a matter of time before the worst happened. Their only chance to protect their warring families was to get to the truth as quickly as possible.

"Underhanded," she said finally. "And very clever."

"With a mother like mine, I'd have to be," he said with a shrug.

Though the ice hadn't broken, she was at least grateful for his company. Even if he was here to keep an eye on her, having his help meant so much to her. For the past several weeks she hadn't spoken much to her family, and with Kirk out of her life she was mostly alone. Sure, there was Jane to help with her store, but that was still a professional relationship no matter how friendly Jane was. And while her brother's ex-girlfriend, Naya, had been generously helping with the investigation by hacking, there were certain things she couldn't tell her. Not without putting Kirk under unfair scrutiny.

Kirk had been the one person she could share everything with. Ironic, considering she had started their relationship with a lie. Then he had forgiven her. Allowed her to be more open than she had been with anyone in years. That was gone now.

At least he was helping, though he'd clearly rather be doing anything else. She'd take that and remember to pay him back for his generosity one day. If he'd let her.

"These look promising." She reached for a stack of folders that were labeled with the months leading up to her father's arrest.

"I've got the paperwork with financial information," he said, holding up a folder. "The folders you have are full of legal stuff. Some of it might be confusing, but look for any substantial amounts of money leaving the legal department. That might shed some light on what was going on back then."

"Okay. Thanks," she said, grateful for his advice. Quickly, she opened a folder and started searching through the daunting amount of paperwork inside.

Now she had to do was focus on what was important. The task at hand. Not hoping for something that could never be. Not despairing over what might have been between them. Not sneaking a glance at him, like she was doing right now. If he caught her gazing at him like this he'd figure out that she hadn't gotten over him. Not even a little bit.

But that didn't matter now. Couldn't. Because, even if he undid the hurt he'd caused and drowned her in kisses, she knew that her shattered heart wouldn't survive.

AFTER NEARLY FORTY-five minutes of searching through documents, they were no closer to discovering anything useful. What they needed was a break, so he instructed one of the maids to bring them refreshments. Soon, they were clearing the documents from the low coffee table to make room for the gourmet crackers, baked brie with figs and walnuts, and the non-alcoholic peach drink she had seemed to love on their first date.

"I would have asked the maid to bring wine, but we need to concentrate and you have to drive back home," he said, desperate to pre-empt any assumptions on her part about the peach drink. Never mind that he had actually requested it because he knew how much she liked it. She didn't need to know that he had committed her habits and her likes and wants to memory. Didn't need to know that it was killing him inside to see her again without ever being a part of her life.

Bethany's presence in his home was ripping his heart to shreds. The part of him that had longed to see her all these weeks welcomed having her here with him, but the rest of him was being crushed by the agony of seeing her this one last time.

They started to eat in silence. When she took a long sip of her drink, a shy smile played on her lips. "You remembered."

"About your love of peaches?" He sighed inwardly. How could he forget? So much for pre-empting her correct assumptions. "Yes."

"Have you ever thought about planting fruit trees on your property?" she asked. "I'm sure your chef would be excited about having fresh ingredients so close by."

Kirk wasn't surprised at her suggestion. She knew so much about fine wine and food and all the benefits of wealth. Not the shallow stuff like flashy cars or yachts. Instead, she enjoyed the things that could be enjoyed for years. He remembered the way her face had lit up on their first official date when she had talked about visiting her wealthy grandmother's orchard. Orchards, and horses, and family gatherings were the things that brought her joy. Then he had crushed her joy when he had left her behind.

"I'll look into it," he said quietly. "Chef Henri asks about you sometimes, so he'll be pleased to hear your suggestion."

"It's nice to know that he still thinks of me." A mournful expression flickered across her face.

The sadness flashing in her eyes sent a twinge of regret through him. He'd give anything to make her smile. He hated being responsible for her unhappiness. For weeks, it was easy to pretend that she wasn't in pain over their breakup. But seeing her now made it impossible to go on pretending. "How's the store coming along?"

Just like he'd hoped, her eyes lit up at the mention of her store. "Things are going great. I've been looking at locations. There are so many commercial properties to choose from, and I want to make the right choice. I want to make sure the boutique is somewhere upscale that gets lots of traffic."

"Glad to hear you're making progress. Maybe someday I'll show up and order another suit."

"It would be my pleasure to make whatever you'd like." Her cheeks turned pink when the word *pleasure* rolled off her tongue; no doubt she was remembering the entire process of making a suit for him the first time around. Things had been far from professional. For one thing, she had kissed him during one of his suit fittings, and then they'd ended up in bed together after he had torn the suit off to get to her.

The sudden heat rising in the room made him reach for his tie to loosen it.

Bethany must have noticed his discomfort because she set her glass aside and got to her feet. "Now that we've eaten, we should take a moment to stretch our legs and get some fresh air."

"What?"

"Come on." She crossed over to him, took his hand, and tugged.

The sensation of her small hand urgently pulling his was a spark of electricity through him. It practically jolted him awake. Seized him so firmly that even when she released his hand to head for the patio, the spark still lingered. The absence of her hand in his sent him to his feet. Without a second thought Kirk strode after her, out into the pale moonlight outside.

Outside, the air was cooler. A sudden breeze ruffled her hair, silver moonlight illuminating her. How had he survived all this time without her? All it took was a moment for Bethany to undo the distance he had put between them. Now, he ached to touch her again. To put his hands all over her until she was quivering and panting, as desperate for him as he was for her.

"I'm going to take a walk," she said over her shoulder. "It might clear my head before we take another look at all those files."

"Bethany, it's dark," he warned. Though they had the light of the moon and the lights that dotted his expansive property, she could still fall or lose her way out here.

"Then it's a good thing I have you around to protect me," she murmured.

He stepped up to her, knowing that he should put a stop to this, but not wanting to. Ignoring the voice in his head that was shouting at him to go back inside, he placed his hand on the small of her back. This was just a walk. He'd stick around to look out for her and that would be the end of it. Nothing more.

Together, they edged around the swimming pool, walking in silence until they stepped out onto manicured lawns.

"You could plant the fruit trees right here," she said.

"There are trees up ahead," he said. "They aren't fruit trees, but it means I've got a gardener I could consult."

"I miss having this much space," she said wistfully. Before he could respond she headed for the trees, and he had no choice but follow her.

When he got to her, she was leaning against one of the trees, her back against the trunk, the branches casting shadows on her face. But even in the darkness he could still see her golden hair, now shimmering in the moonlight. Her eyes glittering as she turned her face to him.

"You'll have space like this again someday," he said.

"Do you really believe that?" she asked.

"I do," he said firmly. "I believe it because I believe in you. I always have."

"Then I hope I don't disappoint you." Her voice was hollow with raw, unmistakable sadness. She shrank back against the tree, withdrawing as if she was worried that she had disappointed him. As if that were even possible. Bethany was too strong and too brave for that to ever be true.

Despite the voice in his head warning him to walk away Kirk took several steps towards her, until he was standing close enough to hear her breathing. Each exhale from her became more labored with each step he took. He lifted his arm to brace himself against the tree as he gazed down at her. "You could never disappoint me."

She returned his gaze, her eyes piercing through him even in the dark. "You're not angry with me? For asking for such an unreasonable favor?"

The urge to reassure her pushed him to capture her chin in his hand. Seeing the turmoil in her was excruciating. For weeks he had been able to go on pretending that abandoning her wouldn't have long term consequences for her. He had deluded himself into believing that, despite being hurt, she'd get over him sooner rather than later. Yet she was still uneasy about angering or disappointing him. Even now, when he least deserved her concern.

"Angry?" Letting her believe that he had quickly moved on from her was one thing. Letting her think he thought harshly of her was another thing entirely. He'd never forgive himself if he let her go on believing that she had disappointed or angered him. "No. Not angry. Never angry."

Bethany reached for his hand and pressed her cheek against it. As if she was just as desperate for his touch as he was for hers. Her eyes closed and she heaved out a shuddering sigh. "You seemed angry when I came to your office. You said you'd changed. You said I didn't know what you were capable of."

Her soft cheek against his palm was already too dangerous. If he didn't control himself quickly he was liable to lower his hand, pry her mouth open, and drink his fill of her. It was dark enough out here for him to give in to his baser instincts. Seclusion wasn't good for them. Wasn't safe.

Maybe he should do the honorable thing and lie. Bury his desire and let her go on believing he was as harsh and cruel as he had let on when she came to his office, demanding he help her. But he didn't have that in him. Not here. Not in the darkness, with her heavy breathing reminding him of every time he had pleasured her. Not with her soft skin on his in a way he never thought he'd ever touch her again.

"The things I'm capable of would destroy you. Destroy us both," he ground out, his voice as hard as stone.

"You've already destroyed me."

Her words damned him. Shock at the pain they caused him nearly made him snatch his hand from her. Instead, he caressed her cheek, needing this contact to sustain him for the solitude that was going to return when she was finished with her mission and out of his life for good. Touching her again was torture. Pulling his hand away would be an even worse torture.

With his heart slamming against his ribcage, he dragged his hand from her cheek to run it through her hair. It was like silk in his hand. Lust for her made his blood run hot. All he had to do was wrap her silken hair in his hand, tip her head back, and take her lips with his. One kiss would slake his lust. And then ruin them both. Undo weeks of keeping his distance and turning his heart to ice.

That delectable mouth of hers was right there for the taking. Mere inches away. She craned her neck to look up at him, bringing her sweet mouth even closer. Her hands found the lapels of his jacket and she held on tightly. Clung to him fiercely.

"You don't get to destroy me again," she breathed.

When he saw the pain flicker in her eyes, he released her silky hair. Turned from her because the pain he'd seen in those blue orbs made it hurt to even breathe. It seemed the darkness hadn't kept anything hidden at all. Instead, it had revealed all the feelings that he had tried to hide from her.

Chapter 4

With tears pressing the back of her eyes, Bethany rushed away from him. Taking a walk had been a mistake. In an effort to take a break and clear the air between them, she had only made it all worse. What had she been thinking—revealing her most secret emotions and fears to him in the dead of night? She had invited trouble. Now she was paying the price.

She blinked the tears away as she raced back inside the house and into the living room. The paperwork scattered around the room dragged her back to reality. This was why she had braved more heartache. Her father needed her to clear his name. Despite the strain on their relationship, she had to help her dad. Her dad had surrounded himself with too many dangerous people and she had to save him before it was too late. If she proved his innocence, then the truth might free him from the wounds of the past.

If she discovered he was guilty...

A painful knot formed in her chest at the thought. As agonizing as it would be, proving her father's guilt would force him to face what he'd done. It might even get him to finally leave the Sterlings alone. Either way, it was now up to her to protect her father. Her own pain would have to wait.

"Bethany."

She heard him coming up behind her, but she didn't dare turn around. He'd see the stricken look on her face and know how much she missed him. Back underneath the shadows of the trees she had said too much. She didn't dare give him even more power over her now.

"We still have files to look through," she said sharply.

When he didn't respond she resumed her seat on the plush sofa and started rifling through files again. Staring at the mountain of paperwork made her realize she didn't know which was worse—staying here with Kirk for another excruciating hour, or delaying the pain by going home right now and coming back to this place on another day. Pain now or pain later.

Maybe there wasn't a choice at all. Kirk always seemed to bring her pain eventually. It always started out with him making her as giddy as a schoolgirl. And then he would rip the rug out from under her and send her crashing back down to earth.

The only thing that kept her from tossing the files aside and storming out was the image of her father being arrested flashing in her mind. Now that she had faced the trauma of her own arrest, she understood exactly what he had gone through on that awful day. Somehow she was going to get him justice, even if it hurt too much to breathe.

Bethany buried her head in a folder, hoping the silence was a sign that he wouldn't press the issue. Thankfully, he sat back down and grabbed a folder.

She looked through documents until her eyes started to burn from exhaustion. It had to be almost midnight. Tomorrow was a Saturday, but that didn't make staying here any longer a good idea for either of them.

Sighing, she decided it was time to go. The tension was already so thick she could hardly think straight anyway. As she started to gather the folders on the sofa, a document slipped out onto the floor. With another sigh she reached for it, her breath hitching as her gaze landed on the paper.

Her eyes widened as she realized she was holding a copy of an invoice. It was an eye-watering amount of money that had been paid to an attorney's office three months before her father's arrest. The logo at the top of the page looked familiar but she couldn't place it. "Benson, Carter, and Company..."

"That's a bankruptcy law firm," Kirk muttered.

"I think this is it," she said, stretching her arm out to hand the invoice over to him. "This must be the firm my father hired."

With a frown he scanned the document, eyes narrowing as he did. "This is the same bankruptcy firm that worked on my uncle's case several years ago."

She gasped. "What? You've done work with this firm?"

"I haven't, but my uncle definitely has," he replied. "My uncle built his fortune after buying out a car dealership. But before he could acquire the dealership he had to settle their debts by signing off on it, declaring bankruptcy. This is the firm he used. I remember it distinctly because my father suggested them. Insisted on them, in fact. He even had me sit in on meetings with the firm's lawyers so that I could give my uncle financial advice."

"Oh, wow." She chewed her lower lip as she thought over his explanation. "It could all be coincidental. I mean, there can't be too many bankruptcy law firms in San Diego."

"There are more than you realize," he said. "This might be coincidental, but it's the first lead we've gotten. If this pans out then—"

"It means your father might be connected to the embezzlement," she interrupted. "I mean, think about it, Kirk. A bankruptcy would have been my dad's motive for stealing all that money from clients. If your father also needed the law firm's help then there's a chance your parents knew way more than they let on."

His shoulders tensed up. "Let's not get ahead of ourselves here." He held up his hands when she opened her mouth to counter him. "And I mean this for both of our fathers. It wouldn't be fair for me to condemn your dad while I expect you to give my own parents the benefit of the doubt."

Surprise made her eyes widen. "Really? This whole time you've been certain of my father's guilt."

"Because the justice system has pointed me in that direction," he explained. "But I did ask you once to let go of your bias. It's time that I do the same. Not just talk about it, really do it."

"So, does this mean you'll ask your father about the law firm?"

"No, it doesn't," he said firmly. "Asking my father about this will make him suspicious. If he figures out that you're investigating the embezzlement and digging for dirt, there's a good chance he'll tell my mother."

"Well, how do you expect our families to find any kind of closure if you aren't willing to even ask for information from your father?" She crossed her arms and raised her chin. Kirk's mother had already taken so much from her family. Bethany refused to let Vivian Sterling take anything else. "We can't let your mother stop us from getting to the truth."

"This is for your own good," he said.

"I'm not a child," she said sharply. "Stop treating me like one."

"I'm not treating you like a child," he said through gritted teeth. "I have to protect you. You know what my mother's capable of."

"Yes, I'm well aware." The memory of cold handcuffs around her wrists brought her to the brink of panic. Several weeks had gone by, but she could still feel the cold metal biting into her skin. Still feel a police officer gripping her shaking shoulders in a painful, vise-like grip. She shuddered. "I'm just tired of letting your parents stop me."

"If she finds out that I asked my father questions to help you, my mother will come after you again," Kirk said, a desperate edge to his tone. "I have to make sure this doesn't get back to you. Putting you in my mother's crosshairs isn't an option."

"Why isn't it an option?" she asked.

"What kind of question is that?" he demanded. "My mother is a danger to you and I have to keep you safe. If she sees you as a threat, she'll do anything to take you down. I refuse to let that happen."

If he thought that explanation was going to satisfy her, he was dead wrong. "Why do you refuse? It's not like we're together anymore. I'm out of your life and you're out of mine. We don't owe each other anything."

"She's my mother. That makes her my problem. My responsibility. I'd do the same for anyone else."

"Oh, really?" Anger that she had been suppressing for weeks flared within her. "You would abandon everyone in your life if you thought your mother was after them? Would you give up your position at the bank if you thought it would keep me safe from her?"

"Bethany, that's absurd," he said forcefully.

"Would you give up your position or not?" she pressed.

"I don't do hypotheticals," he retorted. "I only deal in reality."

"Well, here's some reality for you... You *will* ask your father about the law firm," she said icily.

Shock made him pause for a moment. "I'm the one doing you a favor here. I've let you back into my home. I've put my position at the bank in jeopardy to get you these files and you're trying to pick a fight."

"So this is just one big sacrifice for you, isn't it? I guess you just can't stand to be around me."

"I can't," his said, voice rising.

She froze. Pain settled into her stomach, as corrosive as acid. Dammit, as if the breakup all those weeks ago wasn't agonizing enough. Now she was going to have to hear that, despite his response to her outside in the darkness, he'd still rather be free of her. She was that much of a complication.

"I can't stand to be around you because it reminds me of what we had," he continued. "Of what we lost."

"We didn't lose it. You threw it away," she accused. "You're the one who abandoned me. Everything you said about wanting to make things right for my family after we ended up broke was just a lie."

"This is my way of trying to make things right," he insisted. "Your father paid the ultimate price partially because of my parents. I won't let them hurt you, too."

"Your parents have already hurt me. They took my father from me. Then, they took you." She gulped down some air, caught off guard by her own confession. There, she had said it. The one thing she couldn't take back. Now he knew how hurt she still was.

She couldn't deny her feelings for him after this. Deep down, underneath her anger, she cared about Kirk so much it was a bone-deep ache that she couldn't be rid of. Maybe the wound would heal in time, but there was no way she'd heal while she was around him. Asking him for help had been a mistake. It had put him in an unfair position and was tearing her apart.

Hot tears threatened to fall. Desperate to hold on to what was left of her dignity, Bethany grabbed her handbag and jumped to her feet.

He stood up, reaching out to her. "Wait—"

"I can't thank you enough for all your help. It's just... I thought I could be in the same room with you, but it's too painful." Biting back a sob, she held her head as high as she could and swept out of the room.

———————◦———————

KIRK'S EYES CRACKED open, the sunlight streaming in through the glass doors nearly blinding him. His mind was in a fog, a headache imminent. With a groan he heaved himself to sit up in his enormous bed. The bed he had crashed in last night after Bethany left. Watching her run away from him had been a thousand times more painful than it had been to walk away from her. Because, instead of it being his choice to do the right thing, this time she had thrown his help in his face and left.

After she had left him to stew in his angry confusion, Kirk had raided the wine cellar and drank himself into oblivion. Somehow he'd managed to drag himself upstairs and into his bed. And now, he had one hell of a hangover as a reward.

He groaned again and buried his head in his hands. For weeks he had avoided drinking his sorrows away by throwing himself into work. The one problem with that plan was that last night had been a Friday and there was no work today to distract him. Granted, he was always working in some capacity, but he tried not to make it a habit to work too much on weekends. Which had led to drinking too much.

Groaning again, he stood up and walked unsteadily into the bathroom. When he caught a glimpse of himself in the mirror, he silently vowed to never get drunk again. His face was ashen and his eyes were bloodshot. He looked like hell.

As he muttered a curse under his breath, Kirk turned on the sink faucet and splashed cold water onto his face. What he needed was a good hangover cure. He flung open the cabinet door, grabbed a bottle of painkillers, and knocked back some pills.

With that out of the way he took a shower, got dressed, and headed downstairs. He found his chef setting out breakfast in the dining room like he usually did.

"You're right on time for breakfast this fine morning, Mr. Sterling," Chef Henri observed in his Swiss accent. "A maid has gone to retrieve the newspaper for you, sir. Would you like some coffee?"

"I need one of your hangover cures," Kirk said, sitting down at the table.

Chef Henri's eyebrows shot up in surprise. "It's not common for you to drink too much. Something has happened?"

Kirk heaved out a sigh. Images of Bethany storming out of his house filled him with unexpected regret. He was only trying to do the right thing and protect her. Somehow, doing what was right felt completely wrong. "It's more what hasn't happened."

"Ah. Woman troubles," Chef Henri said with a sage nod. "Has the lovely Ms. Walker forced you to drink?"

He scowled in response. "Ms. Walker hasn't forced me to do anything. I make my own choices."

"And where have those choices gotten you?" Chef Henri asked gently. "Here you are, in this big house, despairing. Drinking to drive the despair away. Why does Ms. Walker no longer visit us?"

"She was here last night," Kirk muttered.

Chef Henri's eyes lit up. "Ah. If she was here, why would you despair? Her presence is like a cool, fresh breeze on a warm summer day."

"Henri, if I didn't know better I'd say you ought to be the one pursuing Bethany." He chuckled in spite of himself.

A mortified expression flickered across Henri's jowly face. Clearly, he wasn't one for jokes. "What a shocking notion. She is far too young. You know, I knew her when she was a girl. I used to work for one of her friends. Even when she was a very rich girl, she was very kind."

"So, you recognized her? You know she's a Livingston?" Shock made Kirk pause. No wonder Henri had seemed so interested in Bethany's wellbeing. There was a history between them. "Why didn't you say anything?"

"Mr. Sterling, such things are not my place." Henri gave him a hard, meaningful stare.

"Oh, really? Is that why you just tried to give me some unsolicited advice?" Kirk demanded.

Chef Henri began to busy himself with piling food onto a plate. "Not advice. I fear I have overstepped. This was merely supposed to be banter, sir. I've spoken out of turn. I will go, and leave you to your breakfast."

Kirk placed a firm hand on Henri's shoulder. "Banter is fine. What did you want to say about Ms. Walker?"

Henri set the plate down in front of Kirk. "Sir, you are the type of man who makes bold decisions. I have this correct, yes?"

"Yes. Someone has to be in charge, and I'm responsible for the safety of the people around me," he replied.

"And what of your safety?" Henri asked. "Who is responsible for you?"

Kirk bristled. He was in charge of his own fate, and always had been. Even if his decisions were dependent one someone else's, in the end he fought for everything he had. "Nobody is responsible for me."

"Ah, so you must be responsible for others, yet no one is to do the same for you?" Chef Henri frowned. "And what if the people you are responsible for do not wish to be watched over so closely? What then?"

"Sometimes people don't know what's best for them," Kirk said.

"So, they are to be treated as children?"

Last night Bethany had accused him of treating her like a child. Now, Henri was saying something similar. He had dismissed Bethany when she said it. Dismissed her and decided her father's fate with a single *no*. Kirk knew her well enough to know she'd never give up on clearing her father's name or, at the very least, doing right by him no matter what that turned out to be. But flat out denying her the chance to dig deeper into the bankruptcy law firm they'd discovered would slow down her investigation considerably. Not to mention the fact that so much of her life had been influenced by other people's choices. Including choices that his own parents had made. She was at the mercy of his family, and he had only added to that by denying her a chance to solve this.

The part of him that was desperate to protect her had taken away the little power she had. Choices were still being made for her by people with far more power. No wonder she had been so upset. Worse, he hadn't listened. Now he was listening to his chef, when really he should have been listening to her all along.

Disappointment in himself made him jump to his feet. "I have some business to take care of. So, I'm going to need that hangover cure. Pronto."

"You are going to see Ms. Walker? To make amends?"

Kirk shook his head. "No. I'm going to see my father. To get the truth."

Chapter 5

An hour later Kirk strode into his father's mansion, brushing past the startled maid who had opened the front door for him.

"Mr. Sterling, wait while I announce you to your father." The maid chased after him.

"No need. Just tell me where he is and I'll take it from here."

"He's in his home office. I really should announce you."

He waved her off. "Thank you. That will be all." Kirk headed for his father's office, not bothering to glance behind him to see if the maid was following him. Nothing was going to keep him from doing the right thing now. It was the least he could do after everything he had put Bethany through.

Kirk knocked on the office door once and headed inside, not bothering to wait for his father's response.

His father was sitting in a leather arm chair in front of the widescreen TV.

"Dad? We need to talk." Kirk shut the door behind him and approached his father.

"Kirk, my boy. I wasn't expecting you here this morning." His father was chomping on a cigar, the overpowering smell filling the room. He looked up at him and grinned, flashing his teeth. His father had always reminded him of one of those great white sharks. Bruno Sterling was certainly as large, sinewy, and ultimately dangerous as a shark, complete with flashing teeth and pitiless dark eyes. "Terrific to see you, son. Now, what can I do you for?"

"It's about Benson, Carter, and Company."

"What about them?" His father's voice remained even, but Kirk saw the muscle in his jaw clench. The tell-tale sign of his father tensing up. Rare for him.

"That law firm helped Uncle Quentin when he bought out the car dealership. They also did bankruptcy work for Lloyd Livingston months before he went to prison." Kirk crossed his arms. "That can't be coincidence."

His father shrugged. "It's business. Familiar faces are bound to turn up." He reached for the remote and changed the channel to a financial news network. "You should stick around for this. Your mother is doing an interview from the conference in Greece. She's going to talk up the bank, which is good news for us."

Kirk narrowed his eyes in suspicion. His father was playing it far too cool. Probably stalling. He didn't know exactly what they had stumbled on last night, but he knew something was up. Sensed it as his gut twisted.

Suddenly, his mother appeared on the TV screen. Despite her difficult upbringing, she looked like the picture of poise and grace as she sat in a chair facing the interviewer. A simple kind of grace that only hard work could have molded.

Even though he was still angry with her for how she had mistreated Bethany, he was flooded with a familiar pride for his mother. Having her as the voice of Sterling Investment Bank at such a prestigious conference was a big deal, and she already looked the part of a business-woman who succeeded at the highest level.

The interviewer introduced his mother, listing her years of accomplishments. "Vivian Sterling, I'd like to thank you again for joining us on the show. Now, my first question is, in light of Lloyd Livingston's recent release from prison, how do you see SIB confronting its past? Has this recent development given you time to reflect on how you took over the bank, or are you ready to move forward?"

His mother flashed an easy smile. "You know, SIB is always moving forward because we are the bank of the future. But taking over the bank from Lloyd's deeply flawed leadership is something I can look back on with pride. SIB believes in transparency, and will continue to build trust with the public."

The interviewer nodded and leaned forward. "Tell us a bit more about how you took over the bank ten years ago."

"Well, it really was a bit of a David and Goliath story at the time," his mother explained. "I started off in the basement of the Livingston Bank. During those years, I worked my way up through hard work and determination."

"Did no one help you during your rise?" the interviewer asked.

"Oh, no. I've never gotten a handout in life. Everything I've achieved I did on my own. Nobody helped me with a thing," his mom replied.

"What the hell is this?" his father sputtered. "*I* helped her. She couldn't have gotten out of that basement without me."

"And who discovered Lloyd Livingston's wrongdoing?" the interviewer continued.

"Oh, it was me," his mother said. "I had taken over the bank and then discovered he had been committing crimes. I was terrified because, even though Lloyd Livingston had been pushed out of the bank, he was still one of the most powerful men in the world at the time. But I had to do the right thing. I had to protect all those people he was stealing from. Once I learned the truth I knew I had to stop him, so I went right to the authorities. Lloyd wouldn't have paid for his crimes if it hadn't been for me discovering the truth."

"*She* discovered the truth?" His father's face reddened and he turned off the television in a rage. "SIB sent her to talk about the bank, but here she is, being her usual narcissistic self. It's not always about you, Vivian."

The only thing that could get his father to lose his cool was, evidently, his mother.

Kirk sat down on the leather sofa across from him and looked right at his father. "Dad, that isn't important right now. What is important is that you tell me about the bankruptcy firm. The truth is at stake here."

"The truth?" His father puffed on his cigar, his face still red with rage. "The truth would destroy your mother. Maybe she deserves it after all these years of taking credit for everything."

Kirk froze. The truth implicating his mother in something shady made his blood run cold. He had always known there must have been skeletons in his parents' closet. New money sometimes had to cut corners to get ahead. But, whatever the truth was, it was bad enough for his parents to have kept it from him for all these years.

"If you want to get the truth out, I'm here to listen," Kirk murmured, choosing his words carefully. He needed his father's trust right now. Needed him to trust him enough to finally come clean.

"That bankruptcy law firm you brought up... Benson, Carter, and Company." His father flicked some cigar ash into an ashtray, his bushy brows creasing. "One of the bank's top clients recommended them to your uncle. They also recommended them to Lloyd Livingston."

Kirk frowned, not satisfied with his father's response. "Okay, so someone recommended some lawyers. How is that a problem?"

"They're a law firm, but let's not kid ourselves here, son. They're fixers. They don't give a damn about justice or the law. If you've made a mess they'll clean it up, even if they have to break every law in the book. They do the dirty work. For the right price, of course." His father's eyes narrowed. "And that price hasn't always been money."

Dread seized him. "What does that mean?"

"It means favors," his father answered. "Favors and bribes. Blackmail. Letting people fall on their swords for the greater good. Working with dangerous people who hide in the shadows. Dangerous people like the client who recommended them in the first place."

"The client... they're way more dangerous than anyone at that law firm, aren't they?" Kirk knew from his father's tone that this client was someone to be feared. Feared because his father feared nobody, and yet his face was turning stark white right before his eyes.

"This client has been laundering dirty money through the bank for years." His father's eyes focused on something in the distance. It was clear he had been waiting to unburden himself and confess the truth for years. Now that he was getting his chance, it was like he had taken such a deep dive into the past that he couldn't let it go. "They laundered the money when it was the Livingston Bank. Then, they laundered money when your mother and I took over. They're still laundering money."

"Why the hell haven't you called the police? You know there's money laundering going on at our bank and you're letting it happen?"

"It's not that simple," his father insisted.

"You and Mom spent years acting all self-righteous because you stopped Lloyd Livingston. You claimed you did it because it was the right thing to do. Because you had integrity." He glared at his father in disgust. "Now you're telling me that you've known about this money launderer for years and you're not going to do anything to stop it? This is insane. If you won't do it, *I* will."

"Crossing this person will destroy you," his father said desperately.

"Did this client put Livingston in prison?" Kirk asked. "Is Lloyd Livingston actually innocent?"

His father scoffed. "What kind of innocent man lets a criminal launder money through his bank?"

"Dad, *you* are letting a criminal launder money through your bank."

"That I am. I'm no innocent either." His father narrowed his eyes. "And neither is your mother. Her little saint act has gone too far. I won't be thrown under the bus. I won't let her betray me."

Kirk paused. Evidently his mother's paranoia had rubbed off on his father. However,, with his father's stunning revelations about money laundering, maybe that paranoia wasn't unreasonable. It was obvious that his parents answered to this mysterious client. A client powerful enough to break the law without any consequences whatsoever.

"Mom might be a lot of things, but I know she loves you, Dad," he said. "She won't force you to pay for things that she also took part in."

Sadness softened his father's hard features. "The things we've done... it's tainted everything. Nothing we have is pure anymore. Not even our sons."

"Dad—"

"Get out while you still can," his father said sharply. "Forget what I've told you and just get out."

"No." He shook his head vigorously. "I won't leave my family behind to face this alone. Tell me who the client is and we can fight them together."

"Never," his father hissed. "I will never tell you. This client has no qualms about anything, Kirk. Right and wrong don't play into the way they do business. When I said they'd destroy you, I meant it. Not in the way your mother does when she sends cops after her enemies. I mean destroy as in *kill*." His father's mouth snapped shut, a haunted look in his eyes. "I've already told you too much. What have I done?"

The fear radiating off his father was so palpable Kirk could hardly breathe. Whoever this client was, they had scared his father so much his old man was unrecognizable. Gone was the formidable titan of financial industry. A babbling, paranoid man had replaced his father.

This kind of fear meant a danger he had never had to face in his life. And if the Sterlings were in danger, then so were the Livingstons. So was Lloyd Livingston, who Bethany had explained was meeting up with shady characters so that he could finally get his revenge. Bethany. He had to tell Bethany about this. Had to warn her. In his desperation to protect her he had almost missed vital information. Information that would actually save her.

Desperate, he shot to his feet. "I have to call Bethany." He rushed out of the office and yanked his cell phone out of his pocket. Adrenaline coursing through him, he dialed her number. It rang without an answer.

"Damn it." Kirk muttered more curses and tried her number again. No answer.

Was she ignoring his calls after their argument last night? If she refused to answer his calls, the only option now was to see her face-to-face. He shoved his phone back into his pocket and ran through the mansion to get to his car. The only thing that mattered now was seeing Bethany. Though he had a sinking feeling she didn't want to see him now, or ever.

BETHANY IGNORED HIS call for what must have been the hundredth time that day. If she hadn't been waiting for a call from her investor, Jane Tanner, she would have turned her cell phone off. With a frustrated sigh Bethany walked down the hall towards her apartment, a laundry basket full of newly washed clothes in her hands. Despite it being a Saturday, she had been lucky to wash and dry her clothes in the apartment building's communal laundry room earlier than usual. At least there was that little victory to celebrate after her terrible fight with Kirk.

Last night had been terrible, and when she had finally made it home she had cried herself to sleep. In the clear light of day she realized she hadn't been fair to Kirk. Helping her with such a delicate matter would put his career and maybe even his relationship with his parents in jeopardy. Yes, she needed his help to keep her investigation going, but he had already done so much for her. Besides, if she was being honest with herself, she wasn't really angry that he had refused to get more information about that law firm. She was upset because he had abandoned her, and clearly didn't see how painful that had been for her until she'd been forced to spell it out for him last night. Just because he could quickly get over ending things didn't mean she could do the same.

You've already destroyed me.

What would have happened if she hadn't said those words? Would he have kissed her? Whispered words she wanted to hear until he seduced her again? Well, after everything he'd put her through, fooling around in the dark wasn't going to be enough.

Taking his call now would only make the situation worse. He didn't want her, and talking to him now was an exercise in futility. Kirk had made his intentions clear, and that was all there was to it.

"Bethany."

She nearly dropped her laundry basket when she spotted Kirk standing outside her apartment door. "What are you doing here?"

"Bethany, I've been a fool. Forgive me." Kirk took the laundry basket from her, set it aside, and then gripped her shoulders. When she didn't respond, he pressed his forehead against hers. "Let me kiss you."

"Yes." The word had barely left her lips, when he pressed his greedy mouth to hers.

He wasn't the only fool. She was a fool as well. After all the pain, she could still be swept away by a kiss. Blazing heat coiled through her as he forced her mouth open with his tongue.

Needing more she surrendered to him, tipping her head back to give him better access. His huge hands lowered to her waist, gripping her until her body molded against his. A fierce, sweet ache pulsed between her legs until her entire being throbbed with it. The kiss was delicious torture. Awakening the passion she had buried when he'd left her. It was dangerous to give in to him like this. Dangerous, and yet her body craved him and him alone.

Their tongues collided and she didn't even bother to suppress a moan. A kiss this bruising and urgent would reveal her desire, not hide it. She clutched his shirt, holding on for dear life as the force of his brutal, beautiful kiss sent her into a daze.

When his hand lowered to tug at her skirt, she broke the kiss abruptly and stepped out of his embrace. Lips still tingling, she narrowed her eyes. "This is it, Kirk."

His green eyes held hers, longing swirling in their depths. "Is it?"

She nodded vigorously. "If you want me, you don't get to smash my heart and walk away again. You don't get to fall for me and then dump me because you're scared or worried about my safety. I'm done playing games." She raised her chin. "Those are my terms. So you can either take it or leave it."

Chapter 6

S ilence was all he gave her.

"That's what I thought," she said bitterly. He was never going to want her. Not out in the open, not as long as their families were enemies. A secret romance was all she could hope for. Sneaking around and meeting in the dark underneath some trees was all she was ever going to get. Secret hotel rendezvous. Stolen kisses.

Except, that wasn't enough for her anymore.

Bethany charged by him to grab her laundry basket. Before she could snatch it up, his fingers curled around her wrist in a tight grip. She huffed. "What are you doing?"

"We can't talk out here," he said, in a tone that unsettled her.

"Kissing me out here didn't seem to be a problem for you," she bit out.

"I have to tell you something." He swallowed and lowered his voice. "Something you can never tell anyone." Kirk shot her a warning glance full of meaning that she didn't understand. "That's why I rushed over here. When you didn't answer your phone I worried that something might've happened to you."

She chewed her lip. His concern touched her. Already had her pulling down her defenses. Dammit! How had he gotten into her head like this? One minute she'd stand up to him, and the next minute she turned to putty in his hands.

Because he cared. That was why she kept coming back to him. No matter how strained things got between them, Kirk always had her back. Always protected her. And she had given him grief for it. Started a fight over it because she was still so devastated about him leaving her.

"I'm fine," she assured him. "Nothing's happened to me." She slipped out of his grasp and picked up her laundry basket. "You can come inside."

Without a word Kirk reached for the heavy basket and, ever the gentleman, took it from her and then headed for her apartment. Letting the silence expand between them, she fished her keys out of her pocket and opened her apartment door.

"The truth is, I didn't take your calls because..." She grimaced. There was no polite way to put this, so she might as well rip off the band-aid. "Because I was avoiding you."

He set the basket down by the door and followed her into the tiny kitchen. "I figured. It's just, after the third call, I started imagining the worst."

There was that concern for her again. The care that had the ability to melt her heart. "Can I get you a drink?" She frowned as she opened the fridge. None of the stuff inside was anything close to whatever fine dining he had at his place. "Is soda okay?"

"Yes. That's fine. Thanks."

She retrieved a cold can from the fridge and handed it over to him. "What's going on, Kirk?"

He popped open the can and took a huge gulp. "It's about my father. And your father. It's about all of us."

Shock made her clutch at her chest. "You asked your dad about the law firm, didn't you?"

"I did."

"You said you wouldn't," she said, barely able to compose herself.

"That was before I came to my senses," he said. "Before someone made me see that I really was treating you like a child." He looked extremely disappointed—in himself. "That wasn't fair to you."

Regret filled her heart. If only she could take back the things she had said last night. She wasn't blameless either. "I know I made you feel like you had to talk to your dad, but I shouldn't have argued with you last night. You were trying to help me, and I let my feelings get in the way of that. No matter how hurt I am, I shouldn't have taken it out on you the way that I did."

"We both screwed up," he said.

"Well, I guess this means you can tell me what your dad told you. And then, you'll leave." Leave forever. He'd tell her what he'd learned and then leave her behind to deal with whatever the awful truth was. The pressure of his kiss was still on her lips. It probably hadn't meant anything more than a goodbye from him.

"I won't leave." He stared right at her, grabbing her attention with just one look. "I won't walk away again."

She fought to keep her lower lip from trembling. "What does that mean? We weren't even really together. We had a few dates and then it ended." It wasn't like they had been an official couple. She had fallen for him while she had pretended to be someone else. Then they had snuck around, hiding from their parents. They had never been themselves out in the open like a regular couple. Everything had been built on deceit. The deceit they had inherited from their parents.

"It means I want to start over. With you." Eyes still locked on hers Kirk set the can on the counter, stepped towards her, and wrapped his arms around her waist. "I'm not going to let my parents stand in our way again. I never should have left you alone." He lifted his hand to brush aside a stray lock of her hair and then cupped her cheek.

The tenderness of his touch was overwhelming. The stroke of his hand across her face signaled his sincerity. His regret.

But she didn't want that. Didn't want tenderness.

As if pushed by some unseen force, she leaned into him until their lips met. Heat coiled through her body. Kirk's strong arms encircled her waist again, his grip on her so tight there wasn't an inch of space between their bodies. They were so close now, she felt the pounding of his heart. Passion was what she wanted, and when his tongue stormed into her mouth passion was what he gave her. His tongue caressed hers, forcing a trembling sigh from the back of her throat.

Even though he knew something she didn't, all she wanted was him. Not whatever his father had said. *Him.* The dark, grim, terrifying truth could wait. Her pent-up desire for him couldn't. That place between her thighs throbbed with need. If she didn't get out of her clothes and have him between her legs soon, she would lose her mind.

Mustering all her strength, she reluctantly pulled her lips from his. "Should we go to my bedroom?"

Pure lust blazed in his eyes. He didn't need to say anything to her. His eyes said it all. And more. So much more. "Lead the way," he said roughly, his voice deep and gravelly.

She grabbed his hand and pulled him along. When they stumbled into her bedroom, she was breathless with anticipation.

Bethany kicked the door closed and paused to look at him. The hungry heat in his eyes nearly set her on fire. She leaned against the door, needing a moment to catch her breath. Though she managed to steady her breathing, her pulse raced.

These last few weeks without him had been misery, and now he was here. In her bedroom. Thank bloomin' goodness she'd taken the time to tidy up her room. If she hadn't, there would have been fabric and thread everywhere.

He held his hand out to her. A silent command for her to come over.

Her stomach clenched, but she boldly walked over to him and began unbuttoning his shirt. Miraculously she kept her hands and gaze steady as she undressed him, keeping her eyes on his.

His skin was hot beneath her touch as her fingertips brushed across his torso while she unbuttoned him. When she had his buttons undone, Kirk shrugged his shirt off.

There was no use in trying to hide her reaction to his bare chest. His tanned skin was golden, contrasting with the dark hair on his hard chest. The muscles of his torso were chiseled, well defined. Wetness pooled between her thighs as lust gripped her.

Kirk didn't bother to wait for her to help him out of his jeans. Before she had the chance to even blink, he was stripped down to his boxer briefs. Then he took those off, leaving him totally naked. His arousal was obvious, the sight sending a tremble through her.

Heart thudding in her chest, she pulled off her dress and tossed it aside. Now she was in nothing but a tiny pair of panties, her heaving breasts exposed.

He reached out to cup her breast, his thumb brushing lightly against her nipple. She moaned softly at his touch.

Flashing her a wicked grin, he took her hand to guide her onto the bed. She lay back, her head supported by soft pillows. Kirk climbed onto the bed and got down beside her.

His lips found hers, heating her entire body. When he broke the kiss he said, "You have no idea how much I've missed this. How much I've missed you."

She arched an eyebrow and licked her lips as she glanced down at his enormous erection. "I think I have some idea."

That made him laugh, the deep, rich sound shooting straight to her heart.

His lips were on her again, kissing a trail across her jaw, down her neck, until he stopped at her breasts. He eagerly took a nipple into his mouth, his free hand thumbing her other nipple. She arched against him, the contact of his mouth on her bare flesh awakening her body. Sending waves of delicious heat through every part of her.

He sucked her nipple, his greedy mouth tasting her until he had her panting.

When he tore his mouth from her she gasped in protest, only for him to take her other nipple between his teeth. Kirk swirled his tongue, licking her like he couldn't get enough of her soft flesh.

Her breath hitched as she struggled to breathe against the on-slaught of his wicked tongue. He pulled back to look at her, his eyes glazed over with the same lust that was now making her desperate to have him. Her patience now gone, she sat up to tug off her panties. After she tossed the flimsy fabric aside, she lay back down and wantonly spread her legs.

Kirk groaned, staring at the bare flesh between her thighs. "You are so beautiful." He positioned himself between her thighs. "I really have missed you, Bethany. All of you."

The way he said her name made her heart flutter. He said it like a treasured possession. Something he would never ever give up. He had promised not to walk away again. But she needed more than his words. She needed him to prove it to her.

"Show me," she said. "Show me how much you've missed me."

His eyes darkened with passion and determination. From that look alone she knew he intended to show her exactly how much he had ached for her. Keeping his lust-filled gaze locked on hers, he thrust into her wetness.

Bliss shot through her core, taking her breath away. With the pure pleasure he gave her, it would be easy to abandon all control to him. But she wanted to show him how much she had yearned for him, too. She lifted her hips to meet his, another thrust sending another wave of ecstasy crashing through her body.

She moaned loudly, the bliss overwhelming all her senses. Kirk started to thrust into her rhythmically, each stroke more powerful than the last.

A soft moan tore from her throat and she wrapped her arms around him, needing his hard body to steady her before she came apart beneath him. Pleasure consumed her as he rocked into her. The punishing pace of his thrusts was a sweet torment she never wanted to end. She clenched around him, milking him until he let out a ragged groan.

More pleasure shot through her, until she was on the edge of release. And then she climaxed, coming undone beneath him. Ecstasy gripped her so tightly she let out a sharp cry. He came right after her with a final thrust, and then he stopped to look deep into her eyes.

Her heart was pounding like crazy, and she felt that his was, too. He was drenched with sweat, his breathing labored as he inhaled deeply. "You're incredible."

She let out a soft laugh and pressed her mouth to his for a brief kiss. "So are you."

He hauled himself off her to lie down on the bed, pulling her close. She marveled at how magnificent his body was and couldn't help but let her hand drift up and down the chiseled planes of his chest. His skin was hot to the touch. The muscles underneath, hard as marble. Part of her still couldn't believe that he was actually here. In her bed.

Kirk brushed her hair back from her face to look into her eyes. "We have to talk."

"About your father or about us?" she asked softly.

"We can talk about us, but I'm not going anywhere this time, I swear."

"Your mother won't accept us, though," she pointed out. "Do you want us to hide again? To keep this a secret?"

He paused, brow furrowing like he was thinking things over. "My mother isn't in town for now, so we have time to come up with a plan. But I don't think we should hide anymore."

"I think we should be private for now, though." She bit her lip. "We do have to think about how the media would react to us seeing each other."

"Private but not secretive," he said. "I can work with that if you can."

She smiled, and gazed into his green eyes. Eyes that she could lose herself in if they didn't have so much to worry about. "There's also what your father told you today."

A troubled expression settled on his face. "I've never seen my dad the way he was today. It was like he was a totally different person. He was scared, Bethany. Terrified."

Though she had barely interacted with Bruno Sterling when her father still owned the bank, she knew enough about him to understand how worrying that was. Timid men did not end up starting with nothing and then go on to own a banking empire. He had a reputation for ruthlessness just like Kirk's mother did. If something scared him, then it was something to pay attention to.

"What did he tell you?" she asked gently.

He heaved out a sigh and slowly started to reveal what his father had told him. Her heart beat faster as he told her the whole story about money laundering that had not only gone during his parents' tenure at the bank, but also when her own father had been in charge.

When he finished, she sat up and pulled the sheets around her. She needed something to shield her from the ugliness of the truth. "My father helped a bank client launder money?"

"Helped wasn't the exact word my father used," Kirk said. "He made it sound like something they had to reluctantly let happen instead of something they willingly took part in."

"But that's still a very good motive for my father's crimes. If someone was laundering money, maybe he started stealing to line his pockets before the truth came out and the whole bank collapsed." She buried her head in her hands as the disappointment made her stomach clench. "And even if my dad is innocent of stealing, he let money laundering happen on his watch."

Kirk placed a comforting hand on her back. "Maybe he was threatened into allowing it."

"My father was one of the most powerful men in the world," she said, dropping her hands. "He was basically untouchable. Who could possibly have power over him?"

"Well, when I was talking to my dad he brought up blackmail. That might be the hold this client has over our parents," he said.

"If blackmail really is the reason, our parents have some serious skeletons in their closet." She wracked her brain, trying to figure out what a blackmailer might have on them. With the amount of wealth the bank generated, anything was possible.

He frowned. "What are we thinking here? A secret love child? An affair? Some kind of crime?"

"Every possibility is terrible, but I really hope it isn't a crime."

"The thing is, now that we have a lead like this, what the hell do we do with the information?" he asked. "I wanted to go to the cops, but my dad shut that down pretty quickly."

"We'd need way more evidence to go to the police," she murmured. "The police were happy to put my dad away. They're not going to like being told they might have to reopen my dad's case unless there's a good reason."

"Makes sense." He paused. "What if I found a way to get the evidence?"

"How? Your father practically stonewalled you when you pressed him for more," she said.

"So, I'll go around him. If he won't tell me who this shady client is, then it's time I figure that out myself," he said. "I unmask the client, and maybe our parents will finally be free. And this war between them will finally be over."

Chapter 7

She arched an eyebrow and shot him a look.

"What's that look for?" He sat up in bed beside her.

Her skin was glowing. Still covered in a fine sheen of sweat. His hands ached to touch her all over. Caress her until they got back into bed and went for another round. Pleasuring her for hours sounded like a much better use of their time right now.

"You said 'I.'" Her full lips turned down into a frown he wanted to kiss away. "You're not going to look for this client without me, Kirk."

He smiled inwardly. Of course he should have known she'd never step back and let him take the investigation out of her hands. Bethany was bold and stubborn. She might let him spoil her once in a while, but she was too devoted to her family to give up on this. "Okay. But if we're going to do this together, we need to come up with some kind of plan. Plus, I remember you were the one who wanted separate investigations not too long ago."

"I did want that before, but us working together got us a lead we never would have gotten on our own," she said. "You were the one who got the bank records. And you got information from your father. I need you, Kirk, just like you need me."

"Fair point. You were the one who brought the tip about the bankruptcy firm in the first place. I had given up on the investigation weeks ago. If you hadn't kept going after leads, we never would have gotten this far." He scratched his jaw thoughtfully. "Okay, we'll work together. I just worry that looking into this client might cause problems."

"That's according to your father, though," she said. "He could be making this client out to be the bad guy to make himself look good."

Dammit. That hadn't even occurred to him. "But why would my father confess all that stuff to me?"

"He might have told you part of the truth to throw you off the worst of it," she said.

"You think he might have revealed something bad to distract from something even worse?"

She nodded. "I don't want to make accusations, but our parents have the upper hand here. They know what they have or haven't done. We don't."

As much as he hated to admit it, she was making some good points. Neither of them could take anything at face value until they got to the bottom of this whole mystery. Still, the thought of his father trying to deceive him was like a punch in the gut. "I don't even know my own parents anymore."

"I know the feeling," she murmured. "I thought I knew my family and now they're all strangers to me. Believing in my dad gets harder every day."

He turned to her. She had been dealing with her family's issues for much longer than he had. Worse, she'd been forced to do it alone. Starting at the age of seventeen. How had she been so brave for so long? How had she not crumbled under the weight of her own suffering?

She tilted her head. "What is it?"

"Nothing. It's just..." At a loss for words, he let his voice trail off. He leaned towards her and took her mouth with his. Teased her soft lips apart with his tongue.

She moaned softly and returned the kiss, her tongue meeting his. Her sweet taste was more intoxicating than wine. He could kiss her for eternity and never get tired of it. After allowing himself to enjoy the sensation of her soft mouth on his for one more moment, he reluctantly pulled away.

"You're the most incredible woman I've ever met," he told her. "I know I've gone overboard trying to protect you, but I don't want to put you in any danger. Last time, cops showed up to take you away from me." His chest tightened as his mind drifted back to the day she had been arrested. That sense of dread lingered even now.

"You helped me get out of jail," she reminded him. "And when my brother came after you I was right there with you, remember? Even through all the crazy stuff that's happened, we show up for each other. I've been on my own for so long, and having you in my life is one of the best things that's happened to me in years."

He gave her a smile. "Guess we've both waited a long time to find each other."

"And the wait was worth it." Determination flashed in her eyes and the expression on her face turned serious. "We do have to come up with a plan to find out who this client is."

"Right. We need time to talk things over," he said.

She grimaced. "I'm still waiting for a call from Jane Tanner. It might be a long call, too, since we're going over so much stuff. Plus, I have to do some last-minute stitching on a dress for a client tomorrow."

"Then we'll talk on Monday," he said. "In the meantime, I'll go back to my place and look through more of those files. I might find another lead."

"Monday might be out. All of next week might be out." She sighed. "I'll be looking at commercial properties for a shop location."

"That's great," he said enthusiastically. "It looks like you're finally making your dream into a reality. I'm proud of you, Bethany."

Her cheeks turned pink and she smiled. "Thanks. I never would have made it this far without you."

"I can't take the credit. You're the one with the talent," he said. "Why don't we meet during lunch on Monday?"

"Okay, let's do that."

"I should probably head out." He gave her another smile and kissed her gently.

Today hadn't gone like he had thought it would at all. He'd woken up with a hangover after a fight with Bethany, and now they were seeing each other again. As impulsive as getting back together might have been, Kirk meant what he'd said. He wasn't going to walk away this time. Nothing was going to stop him from being with her now. Not even the shadowy figure that seemed to loom over their lives.

KIRK SAW HER THROUGH the glass storefront. She hadn't caught sight of him yet, and there was something about seeing her in her natural element. Seeing her made his heart race. Right now she was holding up her cell phone, taking photos of the empty space. Dressed in what had to be one of her own designs, she looked like she belonged in this upscale mall. Her blond hair was pinned up, revealing the column of her slender neck. As she shot photos her lush, red lips turned up into a smile that dazzled him.

He headed inside, clearing his throat to signal his arrival.

She turned and smiled when she spotted him. "You made it."

If there wasn't a chance of shoppers outside seeing them through the glass, he would have kissed her. Instead, he pulled her into his arms for a tight embrace. Kiss or no kiss, he relished having her soft body against his. When he released her, she was still smiling. "The real estate agent is at the back of the store, taking a phone call from the owner. The owner literally just put this place on the market today. What do you think of it?"

He looked around, sizing up the expansive interior. "It's got a lot of square footage. My secretary told me the location was trendy, but I have no idea if that's good or bad." When it came to fashion, he was pretty clueless beyond buying well-tailored suits.

Bethany laughed. "It's a good thing. I kind of wanted the boutique to be elegant with a modern, edgy feel. It's upscale, but for younger clients, you know?"

"Do younger clients have that much disposable income?" he asked.

"Not as much as their older counterparts," she replied. "What they do like are unique items that are affordable. The clothes in the boutique aren't going to be cheap by any means, but the prices will be a lot more reasonable than other high-end stores. Plus, young people are used to shopping online. There's going to be an online component to the store."

"You've done your homework," he said approvingly.

She smiled. "Definitely. And with younger clients, there's the chance for them to grow with the store. That way the base will be younger, but we'll be able to bring in older clients as time goes on."

Pride made his heart swell. Her store was coming along. She had done her research the way he knew she would, and she had the talent to be a real success.

"So, have you narrowed down your choices for a location, or are you still looking?"

"I'm still looking," she said. "This place is definitely going to the top of my list, though."

He glanced around. "Well, I can imagine you having your grand opening here. It's a great space."

Her face faltered. Sadness flickered in her eyes for a tiny fraction of a second.

If he didn't know her the way he did, he would have missed it because she composed herself so quickly. But he'd caught the pained look on her face. "You okay?"

"People invite their friends and family to grand openings, don't they?"

"Yeah. Everyone who supports them is usually invited," he said.

Her face fell. "I don't think my family will be there. They hate me."

It pained him to see her this way. After all of her struggles, she was finally making her dreams come true and her family was missing it. All because she had dared to follow her heart instead of letting other people dictate her life. His pain turned into anger at her family for putting her through this. Bethany had stood by her father at great personal risk. She had supported her wastrel of a brother. Looked out for her mother. Yet, in return, they had disowned her.

"I'll be there," he said firmly. "I know I'm not much of a stand-in for your family—"

"You're not a stand-in," she insisted. "I'd love to have you come to the store opening. That would mean the world to me."

He took her hand and squeezed it gently. "I'm sorry that your family isn't here to share this with you. Just know that I am. And I'm damn proud of you."

Her eyes went all shiny and she blinked rapidly. "Thank you. Instead of letting stuff with my family get me down, I should be grateful for what I do have in my life."

"Plus, you've got your friends," he said. "Jane will bring all her friends. There's the friend who helped you get the lead about the bankruptcy lawyers in the first place. I've never met Naya, but from what you've told me about her she must be a great friend. And even if my mother threatens him, my cousin Ian will show up if I ask him to. You have people in your corner, Bethany. Don't let your family make you think otherwise."

"Hello, there." A well-dressed middle-aged woman suddenly appeared and approached them. Recognition flashed in her eyes. "You must be Kirk Sterling. It's an honor to have you here, sir. I'm Paula Jackson." She stretched out her hand and shook his.

"This is the real estate agent," Bethany informed him. "Paula, Mr. Sterling is handling our investor's accounts."

Bethany had suggested they keep their relationship private, so sticking to business was probably the right way to handle this.

"Of course. It's great to meet you," Paula said to him. "Ms. Walker has such an incredible eye for detail. I knew this was a great space for her to see. And the owner is willing to negotiate a price if you're willing to buy."

"That's great news. Thank you so much, Paula," Bethany said.

"Why don't I give you two a chance to talk while I make a phone call?" Kirk reached for his phone. They were clearly about to talk business, and Bethany didn't need him hogging the spotlight while she worked.

He headed back outside to make some business calls while Bethany chatted excitedly to the real estate agent.

Ten minutes later, the realtor said her goodbyes and headed out.

"I think that went well," Bethany said as she stepped outside to meet him. "But Jane and I still have to calculate if buying or renting is the best way to go with a property like this."

"I'm sure you'll make a good decision," he said. "How about we go for lunch?"

"There's a bistro nearby. Why don't we go there? It'll give us a chance to talk."

"Sounds good."

They headed for the bistro, found a corner table, and quickly ordered their lunch.

"So, now that we can talk, did you find anything else in the bank files?" she asked in a low voice.

He nodded. "The bankruptcy law firm actually had an account with the bank. It's been dormant for years now, but Benson, Carter, and Company were definitely bank clients at one point."

"What does that mean?"

"It could mean a lot of things," he said. "It does show that their relationship with the bank is pretty strong. Or at least it was."

She frowned. "Do you think the money laundering is done through the law firm?"

"It's possible, but I doubt it," he replied. "If this client has been able to launder money for more than ten years without being caught, it hasn't been through a long dormant account. That kind of activity would be too suspicious."

"When did the bank take them on as clients?" she asked, her tone full of meaning. "Was it when my father was in charge?"

He shook his head. "No, they became clients after he went to prison. If anything, this implicates my parents. My father even admitted that the firm was mostly made up of fixers. Now that I know more about them, it's clear that they're not the kind of lawyers an honest person is going to want to hire."

"That doesn't absolve my father, either, though," she murmured. "If anything, this just makes everything seem murkier to me."

"It could actually clear things up in the long run," he said. "Now that we know there's a solid paper trail, we can look for all the connections the law firm has with the bank. That's the key to unearthing who this money laundering client is."

"Does that mean we need more records?" she asked.

"Getting more files from the bank without arousing suspicion is going to be difficult. Maybe you can ask your hacker friend to help us out again."

"I wish I could, but the more I think about this the more I think we need to keep this to ourselves." She sighed heavily. "I'd never forgive myself if I put Naya in any unnecessary danger. I basically asked her to skirt around a few laws, and I don't want to push our luck any further. She's a computer whiz, but this isn't her family. This isn't her problem, you know?"

"I get that," he said with a nod. "You and I are motivated by our families. Involving other people as time goes on might put them at risk."

"Okay, now that we agree on that, where do we even go from here? Without bank records and Naya's hacking skills we've got our work cut out for us."

"Our best shot is to keep looking for connections between the bank and the shady law firm," he said. "Getting hard copies of records will raise suspicions, but I still have access to most of the bank's digital databases. Granted, the digital stuff is for much more recent activity."

"Okay." She paused. "I've kept tabs on my dad in the media for years while I tried to prove his innocence. Now that I have more information, I might find something I missed."

"That's a good idea. Go through newspaper records and whatever media you can get your hands on. There might be a connection hiding in plain sight."

Their waiter arrived and served their lunch—a chicken sandwich for her and a burger for him.

Now that they'd come up with a plan, he wanted to spend the rest of their lunchtime talking about literally anything else. They had only just reunited. He'd rather not spend all their time talking about the fallout from their parents' bad decisions.

"How about we meet up again for lunch later this week?" Even though they both had busy schedules, he was ready to make time for them.

She smiled. "I'd love that."

"And we can go on a date," he said. "One that doesn't involve sneaking around and hiding."

Her eyes lit up. "Kirk, is this the first time we've been out in public together?"

He shook his head. "No. We went out for lunch the day we met, remember?"

"Well, I was kind of keeping my identity a secret at the time." Her cheeks reddened and she took a bite of her sandwich.

"That's right." He chuckled in spite of the circumstances of their first meeting. "If I had known who you really were, I might not have given you a chance. I got to know you without letting my preconceived notions get in the way."

"I never thought of it like that," she murmured. "It was the complete opposite for me. I got to know you even though I made a lot of assumptions about you."

He raised an eyebrow. "What kind of assumptions did you have?"

"I thought you were going to be cruel and horrible," she answered with a grimace. "I figured since you got so wealthy so fast you would have let it go to your head. Let it turn you into an arrogant jerk if you weren't one already."

"You should come to our board meetings. I have my arrogant moments."

"That's different, though. At least, I know that now." She smiled. "You have to be like that when you're conducting business, but when you're away from the office you don't bring that with you. You know when to set it aside. A lot of wealthy businessmen don't know how to do that. I guess that's why I assumed you'd be just like that."

"I'm glad you gave me a chance," he said, returning her smile.

"Same here," she said before sipping her iced tea. "So, where are you taking me on our first official public date?"

"I'm not telling."

"Oh, you're being secretive again. Can you at least give me a hint? Like, what should I wear?"

"Bethany, you look beautiful no matter what you wear."

"Smooth. Very smooth." She laughed softly. "Okay. I know I won't be getting anything out of you."

"None. Just be ready to have an enjoyable time." With all the stress she had to deal with, he intended to spoil her. He was going to romance her and give her everything she'd been denied all these years.

Chapter 8

A few evenings later, Bethany made time to sketch designs in her sketchbook. Talking to Kirk about the shop's eventual grand opening had inspired her with some innovative design ideas that she wanted to get on paper.

Her cell phone rang, and she picked it up from her night stand to answer it. Seeing Kirk's number sent her heart racing. Even though he called her almost every day now that they were back together, talking to him was always the best part of her day. "Hey you," she said when she answered the phone.

"Bethany, I think I'm going to have to let you in on part of the secret," he said.

"What secret?"

"Our date," he replied. "I wanted it to be a surprise, but then it kind of got out of hand."

"Uh-oh."

"It's nothing bad," he said. "Can you swim?"

"Of course I can." Her upper-class upbringing guaranteed that skill. "Are we going swimming for our date?"

He laughed. "No. I'm taking you on a romantic boat ride. Though, for safety reasons I have to let you in on the secret."

"Oh, that sounds wonderful. I can't wait." She smiled. "So, where exactly are you taking me?"

"Nope. That's it. You're not getting anything more out of me," he teased.

"Oh, come on."

"As long as you wear shorts and you know how to swim, you'll be fine."

"Well, what kind of boat are we going to be on? Powerboat? Sailboat?"

Another laugh. "I'll give you points for perseverance, but you're not getting anything else out of me."

There was no use trying to get more information out of him, so she started chatting about her day and listening to him talk about work. So much had changed so quickly. She had gone from missing him so much she thought the pain would never go away, to hearing his voice every day. Plus, they'd had a wonderful lunch together the day before. It was all so perfect that she tried not to worry that their investigation into the money laundering at the bank might throw a wrench into everything.

———————

BY THE TIME THE DAY of their first public date arrived, Bethany had seen dozens of commercial properties and was eager to finally relax and enjoy time with Kirk. He picked her up from her apartment in his SUV and headed towards the waterfront. Finally, he pulled up to the County Water Club and helped her out of the car.

The day was warm, without a cloud in the sky. A perfect day for an outing.

Once she stepped out of the car, he reached for her hand. Warmth spread through her.

Though the water club was pretty exclusive, there were dozens of visitors heading towards the boathouse. There were kids walking excitedly with their parents, larger groups, and couples holding hands just like they were. The date had barely started, and walking with her hand in his was already the highlight of the entire day. They no longer had to sneak around, and being out in public like this made her heart swell.

She held on to him as he guided her up the walkway to the boathouse. When he got everything set up at the front, he grabbed some life jackets and she followed him outside to the waterfront.

The bay stretched out as far as the eye could see, the water calm and placid. Boats dotted the bay and families gathered on the shoreline for picnics. A gentle breeze ruffled her hair, and she pulled a hair band out of her bag to tie her hair up into a messy bun for safety.

Kirk handed her a life jacket. "How about we go choose a boat?"

"Okay. Lead the way." While they both put their jackets on, she followed him as he headed further up the shore towards a low pier. Several white rowboats were tied to the pier. "Kirk, I didn't know you could row. I think this is one skill I never got to learn as a kid."

He reached out to check her life jacket, quietly making sure it was secure. "Don't worry about it. I'll do all the rowing. You can just sit back and relax."

Anxiety settled in her stomach as she watched him grab a line to pull a boat towards them. Getting in didn't exactly look like the easiest task, and with the boat bobbing up and down in the water things looked like they might get a little precarious.

Catching the expression on her face, Kirk took her hand again. "I'll help you get in."

"It looks a little unstable," she said, her voice shaky.

"As long as you hold on to me nothing will happen to you, Bethany. I promise."

She gulped, knowing that he meant every word, yet still terrified that she might accidentally plunge into the water. Gathering her courage, she tightened her grip on his hand and started to awkwardly shuffle across the pier.

"Just remember that boats are meant to float. It might feel unsteady, but it's just moving along with the waves."

"Right." She leaned forward and lowered one foot into the boat. It rocked beneath her, making her flail her free hand for balance.

"I've got you."

The strength in his reassuring tone made her reach for what was left of her courage, and she scrambled clumsily into the boat. It bobbed in the water under the weight, and her stomach knotted up in apprehension. But, like Kirk had promised, the boat remained afloat.

He got in after her, making it look so easy as he took the seat across from her. "You okay?"

She cringed inwardly. If only she could have gotten into the boat with a little more grace. "I haven't been on a boat like this since I took sailing lessons as a kid. I wasn't much of a sailor."

"Something Bethany Walker isn't good at?" He untied the line and grabbed the oars. "I'm shocked."

"Okay, there are other things I'm not good at," she insisted as she adjusted in her seat.

Kirk started to row, sending them shooting away from the pier. "Like what?"

"Lots of things. I can't start a fire like you can," she said, remembering how he had gotten a bonfire going on their first date. Which had been magical. "Honestly, as a kid I liked going out on the water, but I never had the skill for it. I was more into horses and tennis."

"And fruit picking," he said with a smile.

She smiled back. "You know, I just had a crazy thought."

"Those are the best kind of thoughts." If he was overexerting himself to row across the water, he didn't show it. His muscular arms moved in perfect rhythm as he moved the oars back and forth, his biceps bulging as he rowed.

"If I ever make enough money from the shop, I'd love to have a fruit orchard of my own. Or a vineyard. My father owned a winery when I was a kid, and it would be amazing to make my very own wine."

"That's not so crazy," he told her. "In fact, it sounds like a workable plan."

"I doubt it would make much of a profit," she said. "I'd just do it for the fun of it. Maybe people could host events there, too."

"Sounds like you have a new dream to work towards," he murmured.

"I guess I do," she said in surprise. "I've been so focused on selling my own designs that I never even thought about what I'd do after I made that a reality. I didn't even know it was possible to have more dreams." It was then she realized that meeting Kirk had made such a thing possible. Being with him increased her belief in herself. Made her feel like impossible things were within reach if she believed and tried hard enough. Kirk had expanded her world somehow. He'd made her heart grow. Given her so much hope she almost didn't know what to do with it.

"Well, it's a great dream," he said. "I can see it now. Bethany Walker: Famous fashion designer and wine maker."

She laughed, allowing herself to imagine what her future might be like. For so long she had been standing in the shadow of something terrible. Something that she hadn't done, but had been tarnished by all the same. Now, it looked like a new life was possible for her. One where she could design and travel. Have her fashion in magazines. Meet talented people. Win awards. All with Kirk supporting her. He would be the best part about all of it.

"What about you?" she asked. "Do you have more dreams now that you practically run a billion-dollar empire?"

He lowered the oars, allowing them to come to a stop on the water. "I still want to be bank president. Now that I know the things my father is willing to tolerate, I want to take over more than ever. Put the bank back on track. Move on from the shady dealings of the past and be truly transparent. People are losing faith in institutions, and I want to restore that faith."

"And you have to get your father to name you president," she said.

"I thought that's what it would take." He sighed heavily. "But with the way he's running things, there's another way to become president."

"It doesn't sound like you want to try this other way," she said.

"I could force my dad out," he said. "Bring the money laundering to light and take over from him."

"Would you do that?" she asked.

"It's a possibility if he puts the bank in serious jeopardy. But how could I sleep at night if I did something like that to my own father?" He picked up the oars again and started to row, his increased speed making them skim across the water.

She chewed her lip, recognizing how painful it must be to have to even consider a decision like that. "What if getting him out saved the bank? Could you force him out if it would protect people's jobs?"

"My parents forced your father out," he reminded her. "And you hate them for what they did to him."

"I don't hate them."

Kirk stopped rowing again to stare deep into her eyes. "You don't?"

The wind picked up, the breeze caressing her skin. Being in the boat with him made her feel weightless. Like she was slipping across clouds instead of waves. She returned his gaze, letting her eyes lock with his. Her response was clearly important to him. "I don't. Not anymore."

"You forgive them?"

"No," she said, shaking her head. "I don't think I'll ever get to that point, but I'm not full of anger like I used to be. Even though losing my dad for years will always hurt, I haven't thought about revenge in a while."

"Not even after my mother got you arrested?" he asked.

"Not even after that," she said. "Like I said, I haven't forgiven or forgotten. I've just let go of the anger and the bitterness and the hate. I think you have a lot to do with that." She gave him a shaky smile.

He didn't return her smile. Instead, he reached for her hands and held on to them as he kept his gaze on her. "You are the most amazing person I've ever met."

Her cheeks heated and she lowered her eyes to look down at where their hands were joined. Tenderness laced through her for a second, and then, suddenly, her stomach heaved.

She snatched her hands away to clutch her stomach at the unexpected surge of nausea. The salty smell of the bay, which had been so invigorating a minute ago, was now making her ill.

Kirk frowned. "Is everything okay?"

"I think I'm getting seasick," she forced out.

"Do you want me to row you back to shore?" he asked, concern lacing every word.

All she could manage was a nod. Another surge of nausea made her groan. This was so embarrassing. First she ungracefully got in the boat and now she was in danger of throwing up. Their date was going to be ruined because of her.

He started to maneuver the boat back to the pier, each lurch of the boat making her even more ill.

"If I had known you get seasick—"

"I haven't been on the water in so long, I forgot how sick I can get. I'm sorry."

Kirk didn't respond. Merely grimaced as he rowed them back to shore. She had screwed up his surprise and now he was probably irritated. He had probably spent days trying to make everything perfect, and now this.

When they got back to the pier, Kirk leaped out of the boat and reached out to help her back onto the pier. The second her feet landed on the wooden surface, Kirk lifted her into his arms like she weighed absolutely nothing and started to head away from shore.

She gasped. "Kirk! What are you doing?"

"I'm going to find a place where you can rest," he said. "I can't let you walk all the way back to the boathouse if you feel sick."

"Oh." She looked up at him, the determined expression on his handsome face melting her heart. Tenderness made her reach for him and wrap her arms around his neck. "You're not mad?"

He gave her a curious look as he picked up his pace. "Why would I be mad?"

"I ruined our date."

Kirk stepped back into the boathouse and walked into the restaurant inside. Once he walked through the restaurant entrance, he gently set her down and helped her walk to an empty table. He helped her settle in and waved a server over.

Before she could get her bearings Kirk was rattling off instructions to the server, demanding tea and crackers for her weak stomach. He didn't seem to notice or care that her wet shoes had left shoeprints across the restaurant floor.

"Kirk, I have a touch of seasickness, that's all," she protested.

"I've already ordered something for your nausea," he said. "Sit tight until it gets here."

Not that she had anywhere to go to while she was here. Despite her queasiness, she was grateful Kirk was here to look after her.

With a sigh, she took off her life jacket and tried to make herself comfortable while she waited. At least he wasn't mad that she had gotten sick. Instead, he seemed to be going back into his overprotective mode, which touched her in spite of it all.

The server soon returned with the requested tea and crackers.

"Some hot tea to help with your stomach," Kirk said as the server backed away and out of sight.

"Thank you." She smiled weakly and reached for the teacup.

"Wait. Slow down. You don't want to make yourself feel worse," he said.

"Jeez, Kirk, you are *such* a guy." She laughed. "I'm not going to break. I can handle the tea, which I'm very grateful for."

"Okay." He folded his arms, his eyebrows still furrowed with concern. "You didn't ruin our date, by the way. What's important is that you're okay. I can take you home if you want to cut our date short."

That eased her anxiety somewhat and she sipped some of the warm tea. When she was finished drinking most of the nausea had subsided, though she knew getting back on a boat soon would be a very bad idea.

"I feel better, so we don't have to end our date," she said. "We can still spend time together, just not in a boat."

"How about I take you to my place?" he suggested. "It's close by and I can have the staff get whatever you need to make you feel better."

She suddenly felt exhausted, and the idea of recuperating at Kirk's luxury home sounded perfect. "I'd like that. Thank you."

He put some cash on the table and quickly got to his feet to help her stand up.

"You're not going to carry me to your car, are you?"

"That depends." He gave her a hard stare. "How are you feeling?"

"Good enough to walk on my own," she replied.

Kirk smiled, wrapped his strong arm around her shoulder, and helped to steer her out of the restaurant. "Maybe I've been a little over-protective today—"

"A little?"

"Can you seriously blame me for wanting to protect you?" he asked as they made their way to the front of the boathouse.

"I guess not," she conceded with a smile.

It was then that he planted a tender kiss on her lips that heated her all over. Set her very soul on fire until all she felt was warm and *alive*. Wrapping her arms around him to return his kiss she closed her eyes, taking her time to enjoy the sensation of his perfect mouth on hers. She pressed her lips against his, allowing herself to kiss him in a way she hadn't before. This kiss was tender. Intimate. Familiar. As tender as it was, there was a fiery passion beneath it. Something electric traveled through her until she was trembling. Her eyes fluttered open as he pulled way, and she realized what the electric feeling was.

He had kissed her in public. In front of all these strangers. That had been the passion beneath the tenderness. They weren't hiding or sneaking around. This was for real. Not a figment of her imagination. Not one of those wistful, delusional daydreams she'd had after he had abandoned her. They were real. Kirk had just claimed her with a kiss in front of the entire world.

Her heart swelled with so much happiness that she didn't know what to say when he gazed at her. As they made their way to his SUV, her insides had turned to jelly and she was tingly all over.

By the time they got to his place, she was so dizzy from happiness she barely noticed the walk from the walkway to the expansive living room inside. She settled down on the plush sofa.

"I'm going to have one of the maids find some medication for you because I have no idea where anything is in this house. Be back in a second." Kirk ducked out of the living room, leaving her to lie back on the sofa.

She picked up the remote control on the small table by the sofa and started channel surfing. Bored with most of the shows, she pulled her cell phone out of her handbag. Now was as good a time as any to check if her clients had emailed any requests. She checked her email, her eyes landing on one of the news alerts she had set up for the investigation. A new alert about Benson, Carter, and Company was in her inbox. Heart racing she opened the alert, navigating her way to a video that had recently been posted to a local news blog.

It might be nothing, but she had only just set up the news alert a few days ago. This was the first time she'd stumbled onto a video. She played the video, footage of what looked like a fancy cocktail party playing on her phone. For some reason, the party venue looked familiar; she realized that she recognized the huge conference room. It looked exactly like the conference room her father had used to entertain VIP guests when he had been in charge of the Livingston Bank.

The camera panned across the room, zooming in on smiling faces of businessmen and businesswomen dressed in suits and cocktail dresses. Her heart froze when the camera stopped on her father, who was dressed in an expensive Italian suit. He looked at least ten years younger than he did now, with a full head of hair and a wide smile. Two men flanked him, both wearing smiles as they looked into the camera.

"I'd like to introduce Edward Benson from the law firm of Benson, Carter, and Company. He does a lot of good work for some of our clients." Her father's smile widened. "And on my left is Damien Kemp, one of our top clients at the bank. He's the one who recommended Benson, Carter, and Company to me. They're the best law firm in town. I'd be out of business if it weren't for them and Mr. Kemp's recommendation."

The camera lingered on them, and to her astonishment she realized that she recognized Damien Kemp for some reason. She watched as the camera panned away from them and the footage stopped abruptly.

"What's wrong? You look like you've seen a ghost."

Kirk's voice startled her so badly she nearly dropped her phone. "I...I think I've found something."

He was instantly at her side, taking a seat beside her on the sofa. He put an arm around her shoulder and looked right at her. "What's going on?"

"I set up one of those news alerts for the bankruptcy law firm. You know, in case something came up about them. Well, something did. This video looks like it was filmed more than ten years ago, but there's a tape of my dad and someone from that firm." She held up her phone and he took it from her to watch the video.

As he watched, his eyebrows shot up. "That Damien Kemp looks familiar."

"He looks familiar to me, too," she said with a nod. "But I can't remember how I know him."

Kirk handed her phone back to her and scratched his jaw thoughtfully. "Maybe he's a long-time bank client."

"I don't know. A bank client wouldn't get stuck in my head like this," she said.

"If he recommended that law firm to your father, he's probably important," he murmured. "They might be fixers, but Benson, Carter, and Company are discerning. They work with a pretty elite clientele."

"Meaning the type of people who are high-profile enough or successful enough to need fixers in the first place," she said. "A money launderer would probably be in desperate need of a fixer to cover their tracks. That's assuming Damien Kemp is the launderer your father was referring to."

"Right. That's the exact type of person who would need a shady law firm." He nodded. "But if this video was shot more than ten years ago, why would someone put it up now?"

She took her phone from him and looked through the blog for answers. "It looks like a local government website just uploaded a bunch of footage to its video gallery. I'm guessing they're doing a routine update of their website. But I do wonder why a government website would upload footage from some swanky cocktail party."

"It might be one of those local government initiatives that they like to undertake with the private sector," he explained. "Those events are pretty common."

Chewing her lip in thought, Bethany replayed the footage one more time. "I'm going to look up this Kemp guy. There's got to be a reason he looks so familiar." Quickly, she did a search, her eyes widening in shock when the search results appeared. "Oh, shit! Kirk, you're not going to believe this."

"What?"

"Damien Kemp is the San Diego Chief of Police."

Chapter 9

H e couldn't have heard right. His chest tightened. "Are you sure?"
"I'm positive," she said, handing her phone back to him.
"Look, there are photos of him dressed in a police uniform. He looks
ten years older now obviously, but it's definitely the same man from the
video."

Kirk stared hard at the photos, recognition hitting him. "He's been
in the local news lately. That's why I recognize him."

"He has to be the money launderer your father told you about," she
said.

"Whoa, Bethany, think about what you're saying here." He set her
phone down on the coffee table and swiveled to face her. If he didn't
drive home what a risk they'd be taking in accusing a police chief of
breaking the law, she was liable to do something way too bold for her
own good. "We have to be completely sure that Damien Kemp is our
guy. Some video of him with your dad and a shady lawyer isn't evidence."

"I know, but didn't you say we needed to find more connections
between the bank and that shady law firm? Damien Kemp looks like a
solid connection, especially since we now know he recommended the
bankruptcy law firm to my father."

"I'm not saying the connection isn't solid," he said. "All I'm saying
is that we need to be careful."

"Accusing him would be a bad idea," she conceded. "But this might
be a lead. If he isn't the money launderer, then maybe he knows who it
is."

"That makes more sense," he said. "Now that I think of it, I remember a news story about Kemp a few months back. The police depart-

ment set up a sting operation and used local banks to entrap criminals. Some of the cops went undercover and pretended to be money launderers to catch actual launderers in the act. The city had kept it under wraps for months, but some of the details got out. Maybe SIB was involved with the sting. I could look into it and maybe something will come up."

"I remember that story." She chewed her lip. "That could mean that Damien Kemp is a good guy. Maybe he set my father up in one of those stings ten years ago." Her shoulders sagged, the excited air around her turning into something darker. Sadder. "Which would make my father guilty. I feel like I'm just going around in circles, delaying the inevitable. Delaying the fact that my father is a crook who ruined people's lives. Who hurt people so badly some of them committed suicide." Her voice broke and she buried her face in her hands.

The desire to chase her pain away consumed him. Heart heavy, he reached out to rub her back. It was a useless gesture, but he couldn't stand not touching her while she was in so much agony. "We don't know that yet," he said gently. "Remember, we decided not to jump to any conclusions. If you can let go of your hatred toward my parents, I can let go of my hatred toward your father. For all we know, he's entrapped my own parents. Let's focus on getting to the truth and not get ahead of ourselves."

"You're right." She lowered her hands and leaned against him, her body shaking as he held on to her tightly. "But if the Kemp did set up a sting to catch my dad, maybe he can help us get to the bottom of what actually happened."

"He might not appreciate civilians looking into a closed case," he pointed out. "Though, if he's a good guy, we might be able to sway him into giving us access to whatever evidence he might have. Kemp could get us the truth."

She pulled out of his arms and sighed heavily. "What do we do now?"

He mulled over their options, trying to figure out the best way forward. "We have to figure out if he's trustworthy enough to approach with questions."

"So, we have to get close to him."

"That's our best option," he said with a nod.

"Well, how do we do that?" she asked. "It's not like we can just walk into his office and demand he answer our questions."

"No, but we can be much more subtle," he said. "Isn't that what you did when you first met me? You got close to me and figured out who I really was."

"This seems a lot more dangerous somehow," she said. "What if we get close to him and he figures out what we're up to?"

"Well, you got close to me by coming to the bank," he reminded her. "You didn't plan on bumping into me, but you did and you used it to your advantage. We could do something similar. Meet Kemp at a place he's least likely to suspect us of anything."

"Like one of those events that the private sector and local governments take part in, like you mentioned." She scrunched up her face, lost in thought. "Maybe we can organize an event and invite the police chief."

"It's a clever idea, but it isn't exactly subtle," he said. "Our best bet is to go to an event that Kemp is already going to."

"Kirk, that's a brilliant idea." She grabbed her phone from the coffee table, her fingers tapping away.

"What are you doing?"

"I'm going to the local government website." She paused as she slid her fingers across the screen. "There's a special page just for the police chief."

Suddenly, he figured out what Bethany was thinking. "Is there an events section?"

"Yes!" Her eyes lit up. "There's a fundraiser next week and the police chief is going to be there. Kirk, this is our chance."

"We can't go together," he said, hating to throw cold water on her idea. "If we do this, we have to go separately."

She frowned. "Why?"

"For one thing, a Livingston and a Sterling showing up together to such a public event would raise serious suspicions," he said. "Kemp would see right through it."

"You're right. Plus, the media will be there—I don't want to have to deal with a media frenzy just yet."

He didn't blame her for mistrusting the press. Reporters had trailed her for months after her father's arrest. She had still been in high school at the time and the experience must have been absolutely harrowing for her. Kirk was determined to shield her from that no matter the cost. "So, it's agreed then? We go separately?"

"Agreed. Now all we have to do is go through with this plan," she said.

"That's easier said than done." Tension mounted in his shoulders because he knew the hard part of this hadn't even started.

"YOU REMEMBER THE PLAN?" he asked her.

Bethany walked across the apartment living room to lift her hands and adjust his tie. "I remember. Find the owner or another staff member of the art gallery. Chat them up and convince them to introduce me to Damien Kemp. That way it will look more coincidental instead of it looking like I approached him."

"Right. And while you do that, I'll talk to any mutual friends or connections," Kirk murmured. "I'll spend the night digging for as much dirt as I can on Kemp. If someone introduces me to him, I'll bring up the money laundering sting he oversaw at some of the city's banks."

Her stomach tightened with anxiety. After they had discovered the video of her father with Kemp and that lawyer, they hadn't had much time to set this plan into motion. In less than a week, Kirk had managed to snag very expensive tickets to the fundraiser, which was supposed to raise money for one of the city's children's hospitals. Meanwhile, she had researched Damien Kemp, studying up on any detail she could find about his life. With so little time to prepare, there was no room for error. One slip-up could mean that Kemp would be on to them, and they'd lose their chance to get the truth.

Now, Kirk was here at her apartment because she needed to see him before they did this. She couldn't face this without him.

She lowered her hands to take him in. The black suit he was wearing was impeccable. Everything was black, from the shirt he was wearing underneath his jacket to the tie she had adjusted. With his dark looks and dazzling green eyes, the black was perfect for him. His black hair was slicked back, giving him a dangerous air. She shivered. Right now, he was so sinfully gorgeous that for one crazy moment she wished they were going to this event as a couple.

But being swarmed by the press was the last thing she wanted. Better to slip in anonymously. One day, when her designs made it into magazines, she'd court the press and talk about what was actually important. Her work. Not whatever salacious rumors the gossip rags could latch on to.

"You look beautiful." Appreciation burned in his eyes and she blushed underneath his hungry gaze. "Breathtaking, actually."

"Thank you." She slid her hands down the front of her dress, smoothing the deep purple satin one more time. Naturally, the dress was one of her creations—with a plunging neckline and a hem that stopped just below the knee.

Kirk took her hand. "You're shaking."

"I'm nervous," she said. "Once I get into the gallery, I'll settle down."

"Were you this nervous when you were—"

"Trying to con you?" One day she'd be able to discuss that topic without cringing. Regret made that impossible today, even if her lie didn't seem to hurt Kirk the way it once did. "Yes. I was. My family was at stake then, the same way it is now. The truth will finally free all of us, and we're closer to it than we've ever been. I don't want to screw this up."

He captured her chin in his hand, tilting her head back until she was forced to look into his eyes. "You won't. Because you'll do anything for your family. Even if they've turned their backs on you, I know that you will never turn your back on them. One day they'll see that, Bethany. They'll see what I see, and they'll be just as proud of you as I am."

"I don't know how I survived before I met you," she breathed. Hungry for him, she leaned forward to kiss him, the heat of his hard body melting her. When their lips met, she let out a muffled moan. Her arms wrapped around his shoulders as he returned the kiss, crushing her lips with his. It didn't matter that she was going to have to retouch her makeup. She ached for his kiss. Needed his mouth on hers because his touch fueled her. His tongue collided with hers, the demanding kiss turning torrid. He was setting her on fire and she didn't want to let him go. Ever.

As if he could read her thoughts he suddenly gripped her waist, his fingers digging into her flesh. His entire body seemed to be alive with urgency. From his greedy mouth to his demanding hands. When he broke the kiss to rest his forehead on hers, her legs started to shake. Terrified that she might fall under the weight of the passion of their kiss she held on to his jacket, needing him to steady her.

"You can do this," he assured her. "And I'll be right there with you. If something goes wrong I'm a phone call away. I'll get you out of there even if it means we have to break our cover."

His words made her stronger somehow. Strong enough to let go of him and reach up to brush her red lipstick from his mouth. "You go on ahead of me. I'll stay back to retouch my makeup and then I'll head out."

Kirk gave her an encouraging smile. "You'll be the most beautiful woman there." He took her hand to squeeze it. "See you at the gallery."

Once he was gone, she retouched her makeup and smoothed down her hair. Satisfied with her look, she grabbed her purse and headed downstairs to her car. Her stomach tightened again as she got behind the wheel, but she forced herself to keep her mind on Kirk. His words had given her courage and he believed in her.

Steeling her nerves, she navigated the car away from her apartment and headed into the early evening traffic. When she arrived at the San Diego Gallery of Contemporary Art, she parked her beat-up old car around the back and made her way to the gallery entrance. Most of the other parked cars were luxury vehicles. She sighed inwardly. No use in feeling like she didn't measure up to the upper class now. There were more important things to focus on.

When she got to the gallery entrance she found a gaggle of photographers gathered around, taking photos of attendees. Her pulse started to race with apprehension. Eager to get inside so she could disappear into the crowd, she handed her ticket to the guard at the entrance. She could never have snagged the ticket without Kirk's help. This was the kind of event that the city's elite frequented. Which meant that she had been shut out of it for years.

"Okay, you're good to go," the guard said. "Enjoy your evening." He waved her through and she stepped inside.

The gallery was already crowded with the city's elite. Everyone was dressed to the nines and chatting away as they appraised the art on display. As her eyes scanned the space, she found that there were faces from her old life that she recognized. A high school classmate who had ended up being a pageant queen. A former friend of her fathers who owned a local sports franchise. And in the corner, a cousin who was knocking back glasses of champagne while an elderly man spoke to her. A cousin Bethany knew would pretend not to see her. The shame of her father going to prison meant that her cousin was going to remain a stranger to her, even now.

So many people who had once meant so much to her. It was like she was stepping into the past, and it filled her with dread. Made her heart so heavy she could feel it sinking.

A server appeared in front of her. He held a tray of wine glasses out to her. "A drink, ma'am?"

She was going to need something to ease the anxiety. With a nod she took a flute of wine and sipped. "Thank you."

Nerves frayed, she allowed herself to be pulled by the crowd as she searched. She would have to keep her eyes peeled for Kirk, the police chief, or a member of the gallery's staff. Out of the corner of her eye she saw a flash of lavender hair and an enormous pearl necklace. Wilhelmina St. James, the gallery owner. Bethany had never actually met her, but she knew the middle-aged, purple-haired socialite on sight. Wilhelmina was a tastemaker in the city. If she declared that an artist was someone to watch, they became a success over- night. Plus, she was connected to everyone in San Diego. Somehow Bethany had to finesse an introduction to the city's police chief out of the most discerning woman in town.

She was going to have to use every single social grace she had ever learned in her old life. Remembering to smile Bethany breezed across the gallery and approached Wilhelmina, who was standing alone to the side watching the crowd. "Mrs. St. James?"

Wilhelmina's eyebrows went up as she cast her a weary look. It was obvious that the gallery owner was long jaded by the usual small talk from sycophants. "You may call me Will."

"Oh. Of course. Will." She swallowed hard, hoping her tactic to focus on the worthy cause rather than the usual society gossip would win her favor. "Thank you so much for hosting this event here. I'm sure it's going to make an enormous difference for the children."

The expression on Will's face softened a fraction. "I certainly hope it does. Helping the children is the only reason I'd sit through another one of these dull affairs."

"The hospital must mean a lot to you."

"It does. My daughter was born premature and they saved her." Will's eyes went misty for a moment, but she quickly cleared her throat. "I'd do anything for the staff there. Anything." She tilted her head. "I think I know you, dear, but I can't remember your name. Please forgive me."

"I'm Bethany Walker." She felt a twinge of guilt about not revealing that she was a Livingston, but if Will didn't guess right off the bat, that might be to her advantage. It was tough to get people on her side once they realized who her father was and what he had supposedly done.

Will shook Bethany's hand. "Name doesn't ring a bell, but I'm sure we've probably met before. Forgive me if I don't remember you, dear."

"That's okay. You probably meet so many people at these events." Bethany paused to smile. "I love your hair. It kind of matches my outfit."

"So it does." Will laughed good-naturedly. "I must say, that is a terrific dress. You must tell me where you bought it."

"I made it," she said. "I'm a designer."

"Did you really?" Will asked, sounding impressed. "It's amazing. I mean, it isn't the sort of art I'm used to displaying, but it's quite wonderful. Really, my dear, you are an artist."

Her cheeks heated from the compliment. "Thank you. You know, you're the first person I've had the courage to talk to here. These events can be so intimidating."

"Tell me about it," Will said. "But you just need to realize that everyone is more focused on how they're coming across rather than what anyone else is doing. Maybe I can introduce you to some fashionistas."

"Well, I think I'd be more comfortable meeting city officials," Bethany blurted out.

Will's eyebrows went up again. "City officials?"

"Yes. That way I won't be talking about my designs all night. Wouldn't want to look like I came to this event to network." Bethany forced herself to smile, hoping Will would accept her excuse.

"Of course. Well, who would you like to meet? How about the mayor? He's a bit dull, but he's nice."

"What about the police chief?" Bethany asked. "I'd love to congratulate him on his recent police sting."

"Sure, he's over at the *Girl with Bird* painting," Will murmured, pointing at a painting of two huge orange blobs.

Bethany's heart raced when she spotted Damien Kemp, who was dressed in his police uniform and talking to another officer dressed in police uniform.

Will linked her arm with hers and guided her across the gallery to the police chief. "Mr. Kemp. May I introduce Bethany Walker? She's been dying to meet you."

"Well, I wouldn't say dying—" Bethany blinked in amazement as she realized that Will and the officer beside the police chief had already disappeared into the crowd. "I think Wilhelmina meant that I've been looking forward to meeting you."

"That's surprising," the police chief murmured, his voice low but distinctively clear. "Especially since, as a Livingston, you've had so many brushes with the law."

Chapter 10

She nearly dropped her wine glass in surprise. "How did—"
"How did I know you're Lloyd and Cybil Livingston's daughter?" The police chief looked down his nose at her, his jaw tightening. "What kind of cop would I be if I didn't recognize you?"

Her lungs constricted. This wasn't part of the plan. He wasn't supposed to recognize her. Not with the number of people he must know and ten years passing since her father's arrest. Crap, he'd probably sized her up already and figured out that she wanted answers from him.

Resolve shattered, she fished her phone out of her purse with trembling hands. Kirk. She needed Kirk. He'd know how to salvage this situation.

Her eyes darted across the room until she spied Kirk deep in conversation with the mayor. Kirk must have found a way to ask the mayor about Damien. Which meant his part of the plan was probably working. If he was doing everything he could to see this through, she was going to have to gather her courage and at least figure her way out of this.

"Ms. Walker? Are you okay?"

She stilled her hands long enough to look up at him. Instead of the contempt she expected to see in his eyes, she saw concern. Based on her research she knew that, at the age of forty, Damien Kemp had become the city's police chief. He'd been ambitious all his life, working his way up through the ranks of the police force with a series of daring, high-profile arrests. None of those arrests had involved her father, but from the video she had seen she knew that Damien had known her father all those years ago.

"I'm fine," she said.

"I've been rude, haven't I?" Damien took off his cap and ran his hand through his graying brown hair. The gray gave him a rugged, grizzled appearance. Looking at him now she realized that the police chief was actually quite handsome, with intense dark eyes and a strong jaw. "Please forgive me. I was trying to make a joke like my PR officer was suggesting and I've offended you."

"It's okay—"

"No, it's not okay. I made a tasteless joke at your expense and I feel lousy about it," Damien said. "I won't blame you if you fling your drink in my face and storm off."

"I wouldn't do that," she said, assuring him with a faint smile. "Why did your PR officer suggest you make a joke?"

"He says that when the topic isn't police work, I come across as stiff and intimidating. He seems to think that I only know how to talk about police work." The police chief grimaced and put his cap back on. "I'm Damien Kemp, by the way."

"I know who you are," she reminded him.

"Right. And I know who you are."

A tense silence passed between them. Damien pinched the bridge of his nose. "I've done it again. Please forgive me. I meant, I'm sure your happy that your father has finally been released. And I meant that I learned about your recent arrest from one of our officers and I'm glad it seems to have been sorted out."

"Thank you. I'm happy that my father is finally home," she said. "Did you know him, Chief Kemp?"

"Please, call me Damien," he insisted with a smile. "I did know him. The city kept police pension funds at the Livingston Bank and officers had bank accounts with them. I got to know your dad when I opened my account at the bank. He had been supportive of city employees and we became pretty friendly. Unfortunately, I discovered that he had ulterior motives for encouraging city employees to open accounts at his bank."

Her chest tightened. "Did you lose money because of what they say my father did?"

"I did," he said in a grim tone. "Quite a bit of money that I had saved up, actually. But once the Sterlings got the bank back on track and rebranded, they helped me salvage some of what I'd lost. The Sterlings saved me from ruin, though things have been rocky from time to time. Anyway, I was one of the lucky ones. I guess my account was small potatoes compared to charity groups and such."

Mentioning the Sterlings made her stomach do somersaults. It reminded her that she had to be on her guard. This wasn't a friendly chat with the chief of police. She had to figure out if there was more to Damien's connection to her father and the bank. Had to know if he had laundered money and why. To set up criminals? Or to line his own pockets? If things had been rocky between him and Kirk's parents, maybe there was more to the story.

So far he seemed to have been caught up in actually losing money to the embezzlement, which was a piece of the puzzle they hadn't had before. Losing his savings to a man he had befriended must have felt like a betrayal.

"I'm sorry," she said softly.

Surprise flashed in his eyes. "It isn't your fault. And things must have been very difficult for you at the time. I'm amazed you didn't leave town to start over. You're incredibly brave, Ms. Walker."

"Please, call me Bethany."

He smiled at that and gazed into her eyes. "Such a beautiful name."

"Thank you," she said.

"I know that the circumstances of our lives haven't been easy, but I'm glad we've finally met," he said. "It's good to see that Lloyd Livingston's daughter turned out to be such a lovely young woman."

"That's so kind of you to say. Thank you."

He seemed to relax slightly and smiled. "You're the first person I've felt comfortable talking with tonight. You're a miracle worker, Bethany Walker."

She laughed. "I don't know about that. It's been nice to talk to you, though. Big events can be nerve-wracking, and yet you've put me right at ease."

"In that case..." He stood up even straighter and cleared his throat. "I know this is unorthodox, and you can always throw your wine at me if I overstep, but I'd like to take you out for a coffee if that's okay."

"Oh. As in..."

"As in a date," he said. "There's a coffee place just across the street and I'd be honored if you'd join me."

His words stunned her. From her research she knew that Damien was single, but she hadn't expected him to be interested in her like this. She had no romantic interest in Damien whatsoever, but maybe she could use his interest in her to finally solve this decades-old mystery. "You mean go on a date right now?"

"I've overstepped. I knew it. You probably have a boyfriend or—"

"No, I don't have a boyfriend," she said sharply. The lie rolled off her tongue so quickly the pain of it shocked her. In her desperation to protect Kirk and get closer to the police chief she had blurted out a lie.

"Of course," he said. "If you did, I doubt he'd let you come here all alone. Well, if you'd rather not, I understand. I'll likely stay here for a few more minutes for appearances' sake and then head out."

"You'll leave?"

He nodded.

If he left she might miss her only chance to find out the truth. Having coffee with him wouldn't hurt. She'd just share a drink with him while she gathered intel. Kirk was probably getting a ton of information from the mayor. She didn't want to disappoint by coming back empty-handed. Besides, the police chief had mentioned the Sterling family. This was her chance to find out more. "Sure, I'd love to have coffee with you."

———◉———

HIS PHONE BUZZED AND he held up his hand to interrupt Mayor Howard while he retrieved it from his pocket. Bethany might be desperately trying to get in touch with him.

Kirk turned his back on the black-and-white photograph he and Mayor Howard had been admiring and checked his messages. There was a new one from Bethany.

"*Made contact with Kemp! Gone out for a minute with him for more info.*"

He frowned. Leaving the gallery hadn't been part of the plan. And he sure as hell hadn't agreed to her going with Kemp. Considering Kemp's police work, Kirk was starting to believe they could trust him. But if they were wrong, he didn't like the idea of Bethany going off somewhere with the man.

"Will you excuse me for a moment, Your Honor?" he asked. "Something has come up."

"No problem. We'll talk when you get back," Mayor Howard said with a nod.

Based on what Mayor Howard had revealed, Kemp had lost money to Lloyd Livingston's embezzlement scheme. It was a clue that might end up being useful, and he knew they were going to have to stick to their plan if they wanted to get to the truth.

Needing to make sure she was okay, he fired off a response to her message and pushed his way through the crowd. Finally, he got outside to ask the guard out front if he had seen Bethany or the police chief.

The guard gave him an apologetic shrug. "I saw them leave, but I didn't see where they were headed."

Kirk grabbed his phone again to check if Bethany had responded. So far, no response. Concern for her started to give way to worry. What if the police chief had figured out what she was up to? He might use his considerable power to send her to jail.

Chest tightening, Kirk headed up the sidewalk, keeping an eye out for Bethany. Why hadn't she just stuck to the plan? Hadn't he told her he'd be a phone call away? Hadn't he told her that he would always believe in her? There was no reason for her to be so reckless. Agreeing to go through with something this dangerous had been a mistake. He knew that now. If only he could find her.

When he glanced across the street, he stopped dead in his tracks. There she was. He could see her through the huge coffee shop window. And she wasn't alone. Damien Kemp was sitting across from her, gazing longingly into her eyes. She was laughing at something he said.

What came next devastated Kirk. Sent him into turmoil as dark, contradictory emotions swirled inside him. Indignation. Anger. And pain that cut through him like a blade through bone. Damien was holding on to her hand, and then he brought her hand up to his lips to kiss it.

RAGE AND JEALOUSY TORE at his insides. Bethany and the police chief looked like lovers sharing a romantic evening. As Damien Kemp held her hand to his lips for a long moment, she smiled. She actually smiled. And then leaned closer, as if she was enjoying his company. His touch.

Kirk balled his hands up into fists, the urge to strike the police chief unshakable. Damien was touching her like they had known each other for years. The familiarity of it made Kirk take a step forward, his foot hitting the asphalt of the street. He could cross the street in seconds, storm into the coffee shop, and give Damien the thrashing he deserved.

But violently confronting the chief of police right now would backfire. The consequences of letting his anger get the best of him were enormous. Especially when the mayor and most of the city's press were just a few feet away inside the gallery. Worse, getting violent during a charity for a children's hospital would ruin him. He'd drag his family name through the mud and put a serious dent in Sterling Investment Bank's reputation.

On top of all that, he would drag Bethany back into the headlines. Her shop was going to open in the near future. If she ended up being gossip fodder before she even launched, her career would be destroyed. Ruined beyond repair. As angry and devastated as he was at seeing her looking so cozy with Damien, he couldn't derail her dreams. His heart wouldn't let him.

Still shaking with rage, he slowly unclenched his fists and turned around. Though he wanted to get away from the stifling gallery, he couldn't just leave without telling Mayor Howard. The mayor had been helpful. It was best to at least say goodbye to him. He would face Bethany later. And then, when the time was right, he would make Damien Kemp pay for overstepping.

Kirk headed back inside and found Mayor Howard talking to some city officials.

"You're back," Howard said. "That wasn't an emergency, I hope. You kind of took off in a hurry, Kirk."

"I have to leave," Kirk explained.

Howard frowned and signaled to the officials around him to leave. Without the mayor even having to say a word the city officials all scattered, giving them privacy.

"This sounds serious. Is this something I can help with?" Mayor Howard asked.

"It isn't about business. Best not to involve you in my personal life," Kirk replied. "It's been good catching up with you, though."

"This personal issue wouldn't have to do with the police chief, would it?"

Stunned, Kirk's eyebrows shot up. "How did—"

"You've subtly asked me about Damien Kemp all night," Howard said. "I don't know what's going on, but if it's personal I want to give you some advice." Howard's expression darkened. "I know I offered my help, but if you've gotten on Damien's bad side I can't help you."

Kirk couldn't believe what he was hearing. The mayor was warning him about his own police chief. "It sounds like you're afraid of him, Mayor."

"I'm not afraid of anyone," the mayor said, indignant. "I just know that there are some people I can't defeat. Not without it blowing back on me."

"Why would you want to defeat your own police chief?" Kirk asked in disbelief. "Doesn't Damien answer to you?"

The mayor frowned. "I respect you, so I'm going to give you some friendly advice. If you're taking Kemp on for some reason, you had better make sure it's worth it."

"Trust me. She's worth it." Leaving the mayor to deal with the shock on his own, Kirk turned around on his heel and sauntered out of the gallery. He'd already made a generous donation to the local children's hospital. Sticking around would just make the situation boil over until he publicly confronted Damien Kemp and caused a scene. Best to get the hell out of there before his anger got the best of him.

As he stewed in his mounting rage, Kirk stepped back outside and looked across the street. His stomach dropped as he saw Damien feeding Bethany from whatever was on his plate. The sight of the woman he cared so much about batting her eyes at this man was torture. He had to get out of there. And fast. He rushed to his car and got into the driver's seat. He took out his phone and sent a message to Bethany, letting her know that he would wait at her apartment. Part of him wanted to call her to demand just what she thought she was doing by throwing herself at Damien, but that would only escalate things. A message was the right call.

He didn't know if she was leading Damien on to get information out of him, or if she was ready to be unfaithful to him. Either way, that was the kind of conversation they needed to have face-to-face.

With the message sent, he stepped on the gas and sped away to her apartment.

When he arrived, Kirk pulled in to the apartment building's parking lot. They hadn't actually made a plan for where to meet after the fundraiser. It seemed safer to go their separate ways at the end of the night and meet up tomorrow. That way, they'd reduce the chance of being seen together after such a public event. Now he was here. Too agitated to go home.

Seeing Bethany like that with another man was dragging him into a pit of despair. He had never felt this way about a woman, and getting control of his feelings was futile when it came to her. No matter how deep he buried something, she always brought it to the surface. There was no hiding with her. At least, not for long.

He waited in the car for ages. Watching the minutes tick by until it was past midnight. As time went on, his thoughts got darker and darker. His anger at Damien and his disappointment in Bethany getting worse.

The low rumble of a car engine dragged him from his grim thoughts, and he glanced out the car window. Bethany's car pulled in on the other side of the parking lot.

Needing to confront her, Kirk shot out of his car and sauntered over to her.

When she opened the door and stepped out, the lights overhead lit up her golden hair. Even in the harsh glare, her beauty was unmistakable.

She froze when she spotted him, her mouth falling open. "*Kirk.*" Her gaze turned from him, back to her car.

It was then that Kirk realized that there was someone else in the car. A man dressed in a police uniform.

Chapter 11

She had never seen Kirk look so angry. So devastated and hurt. Pain flickered in his eyes, but anger hardened the expression on his face. His mouth twisted in pure disdain.

Bethany followed his gaze and realized he was looking right at Damien.

Glancing back at Kirk in confusion she stood frozen in place, not knowing what to do. After her conversation with the police chief went nowhere useful, she had gone back into the gallery. She had searched for Kirk, unable to shake Damien, who didn't seem to want to leave her side. Eventually, she realized that Kirk must have left. By then, her phone had died and she couldn't very well ask for someone else's phone to contact Kirk. Not if they wanted to keep a low profile.

That was when she had decided to come home to call Kirk from her apartment, but Damien had insisted on seeing her safely home. The only problem was, she hadn't expected to see Kirk here. She had mistakenly assumed that he had left the fundraiser early to deal with some unexpected bank business.

"You brought him home with you?" Kirk thundered.

Her heart thudded against her ribs, panic rising inside her. "Kirk, listen—"

"I saw you with him at the coffee shop," Kirk accused. "You two looked *very* cozy. A little too comfortable."

"No. It wasn't like that," she insisted. Her heart was beating so fast, it was a struggle to get the words out. Hurting him was the last thing she wanted to do, but it was obvious that she had failed.

"I trusted you," Kirk said with a growl.

"And I trusted you."

She whirled around at the sound of Damien's voice. The police chief was stepping out of the car, a sinister shadow darkening his face.

"Clearly, that was a mistake." His voice was deceptively smooth. Dark and low, with a warning underneath. The polite, affable police chief was now gone. In his place stood a man who was so eerily calm it sent goose bumps across her skin. Damien took a menacing step towards her, making her shrink back instinctively. "I should have known that Bethany Walker would turn out to be as deceitful and conniving as her father."

In the blink of an eye Kirk stepped in front of her, positioning her behind him as he shielded her with his body. "Watch your mouth."

Momentary surprised flashed in Damien's eyes, but he recovered quickly. "How did I miss it? A Livingston and a Sterling can't be under the same roof without it turning into a fight. Yet there you two were at the gallery. At the same event, and not so much as a harsh word exchanged between you. Odd. And now you're both here together, looking more than a little friendly. You two are obviously in on something."

"This is none of your business," Kirk said with a growl. "Get the hell out of here or I'll—"

"Or you'll do what?" Damien spat out, cutting him off. "Call the cops?" He laughed humorlessly. "You Sterlings really think you're above the law now that you've made it. Well, you're not."

"Neither are you," Kirk shot back.

Another humorless laugh. "I'm the chief of police. I am the damn law."

Her legs began to shake. If she didn't break this up, one of them was going to get hurt. This was her fault. If she had stayed in the gallery and declined Damien's request for a date, none of this would be happening right now. She had to fix this somehow.

"Damien, please go home," she begged. "You helped me get home safely and I'm grateful. But you really should go now. It's getting late."

"Not until you tell me what the hell is going on," Damien said icily. "First you tell me that you don't have a boyfriend, and now Kirk Sterling shows up at your place, acting like a jealous lover. I want the truth. Now."

"The truth is you need to get the hell out of here." Kirk balled up his hands. "And stay away from my girlfriend."

He had never referred to her as his girlfriend before. Hearing him claim her even now made her bruised heart soar. After all this time, Kirk saw her as his. If only she hadn't been so foolish. She'd been so focused on getting the truth about her father that she had disrespected what they had. Risked it all so that she could end the feud between their families. What use was peace between their families if she had caused Kirk so much pain?

Damien narrowed his eyes. Eyes that had started off concerned and friendly, but were now cold and pitiless. "I came all this way with her to see her home safely. The least I deserve is an explanation. Unless... there's a reason you're keeping the truth from me."

She tried to step in front of Kirk to try to reason with Damien, but Kirk gently blocked her with his arm. "Kirk, let me try to talk to him."

"No way," Kirk said through clenched teeth. "He's not going to listen to reason."

"You two are working together, aren't you?" Damien crammed his hands into his pockets and glowered. "That's the only thing that makes sense. A Livingston and a Sterling would only get together if there was some kind of mutual benefit. Which means you both want the same thing. *Me.*"

Silence. Nobody said a word as Kirk threw his shoulders back, like he was ready to do something crazy.

"You came to the gallery because you knew I'd be there," Damien continued. "So, what do you want? What lies have you heard about me?"

"We know that you're up to something," Kirk said coldly. "You launder money through the bank. Don't try to deny it."

Damien stiffened visibly for a split second before relaxing again. "The police department sometimes relies on banks to lure criminals. We set up stings by pretending to launder money through the bank. That's well known."

"Why go to the bank where you lost your money?" Bethany asked, refusing to let him off the hook. She could sense that they were on to something from the way the police chief deflected Kirk's accusation so fast. "You told me earlier tonight that my father stole your money. Most of the people my father stole from left the bank and didn't stick around when the Sterlings were in charge. That's why the Sterlings keeping the bank afloat through all that was such a big deal. They brought in new clients after all that scandal. Kept the bank from crashing and going bankrupt. So, why did *you* decide to do police work with the same bank that had nearly gone under because of scandal? Seems kind of reckless for a police officer to be so trusting."

"The Livingston Bank is the Sterling Investment Bank now, and has been for years. The bank changed hands and that was enough for me," Damien replied quickly. Too quickly. "The Sterling family had a good enough reputation by then. I figured doing police work with them would work out, despite your father's embezzlement. You should be careful flinging around accusations, Bethany. After all, you're the one with a criminal for a father."

"Her father isn't the one on trial here," Kirk said with a growl. "Livingston has paid for his part in whatever this is. You, on the other hand, have a lot to answer for."

"I wouldn't listen to unfounded rumors if I were you," Damien threatened. "You'll end up chasing after stories that you shouldn't."

"What's the matter?" Kirk demanded. "Scared of what we'll find? If your money laundering is above board, why don't we talk to your police department about it? Or let the mayor in on it?"

"I'm warning you, Sterling..." Damien took another menacing step towards them, his jaw clenching. "Mind your own damn business."

Kirk snarled. "Or what?"

"Or you're liable to end up just like Lloyd Livingston did," Damien shot back. "Rotting away in prison."

She hated the arrogance in Damien's tone. Clearly, he knew something about her father. But accusing him wasn't going to work. He'd hide and deflect. Or worse, try to bully and intimidate them into silence. There had to be another angle. Another way to get Damien off guard enough to spill his secrets.

After she had managed to hide her identity from Kirk for weeks, she knew she could think on her feet when the time called for it. "Oh, please," she said loudly. "You expect us to believe that? Now that I've seen you face to face, Damien, I'm starting to have second thoughts. There's no way you had anything to do with my father going to prison. You don't have what it takes to pull that off. Men like you don't put men like my father in prison."

"You're wrong." Damien bared his teeth, the calm menace slipping away. "You Livingstons needed to be taken down because you kept getting in the way. Your family did everything to keep the new-money businessmen out. The type of businessmen who gave me a chance. Who saw something in me and got me into the police academy."

Her pulse quickened at the implication of what he was saying. The type of businessmen he was talking about weren't the sort who worked within the confines of the law. Average businessmen didn't put people on police forces. Only shady people who needed cops in their pockets did things like that. Only the most dangerous men connected to organized crime could take risks like that. "Those people weren't businessmen," she said sharply. "They were criminals and you know it. My father was right to shun those people."

Damien's expression hardened. "I was one of those people. Those businessmen got me off the street and taught me to be a real man. Not some rich asshole who inherited everything. I worked my way up from running errands to—" He stopped short, his eyes darting around in suspicion.

"To what? Getting stolen goods off trucks? Drug deals? Extortion? Money laundering?" Kirk demanded. "Or did you graduate to something worse, Kemp? What kind of sick crap did you do for these people?"

"Whatever it took. I'm not going to apologize for having the balls to do what had to be done."

"So you're just a hired gun. A lackey for shady criminals," Kirk muttered. "I should have known. You don't have a mind of your own. No wonder you targeted Lloyd Livingston. He was everything you weren't. He was the type of man who didn't have to answer to anyone, and you couldn't stand that."

She gripped Kirk's shoulders, realizing that he had probably caught on to the way she had baited the police chief earlier.

"That's crap. I'm the one who kept Livingston afloat all those years. He answered to me. Me. I started off as an errand boy for the businessmen Lloyd and his type look down on. Maybe I started working for them, but when they got me into the police academy I was their equal. I didn't have to be an errand boy for them anymore. They don't keep men down once we've proven ourselves. When I became a cop, I got real power. Enough power to have Lloyd in the palm of my hand."

"That's a lie," she countered. "You couldn't control my father."

Damien laughed. "Oh yes, I could. Once I got into the police academy, I met your father. Got into his good graces. The men I worked for couldn't wield power directly. They needed a powerful stooge in their pockets and your father fit the bill perfectly. He trusted me so much that he came to me for a loan. Then he came to me for even more loans."

Her eyes widened. "Why would my father come to you for loans? He was one of the richest men in the country." This time she wasn't bluffing. Damien's words had gotten under her skin.

"Because he pissed all his money away. He wasn't the financial genius he pretended to be. That's the problem with inherited wealth. If you've never had to earn it, or bleed and sweat for it, you never learn how to hold on to it. Your father lost so much money to bad investments, and that's when I knew I had a way in. The people I work for needed a powerful man they could control. That man was your father." The terrifying smile on Damien's face chilled her to the bone.

"You targeted my dad on purpose," she whispered.

"All that power and he was still so weak. He was desperate for money by the time I befriended him. I was happy to oblige. Even though the businessmen I work for don't have as much power and influence as the old families in town they had money to spare, so they loaned him money. A lot of money."

"So the family wealth was..." She swallowed hard as she tried to piece together all the unsettling details.

"It was all built on a house of sand." Damien's smile widened, turning triumphant. "He pissed it all away and could only prop up his crumbling empire with loans from my bosses. Loans from the types of people you Livingstons look down on. How does it feel, Bethany? To know that all that money you took for granted came from people you turn your nose at? People you judge for getting rich by doing whatever it took while you upper- class frauds cut corners to keep your wealth?"

"Did my father cut corners?" she demanded breathlessly. "Is that what you're saying? That he stole all that money?"

Something cruel flickered in Damien's eyes. "That's what this is about." His mocking laughter cut through the night, echoing across the parking lot. "You're trying to find out just how bad your father is. Is he a crook? Was he set up? Is he innocent?"

Only the truth could set them all free. The truth could finally give their families peace. Closure after all these years of pain. She knew it was the only way to save her family. "Tell me."

"No." Damien shook his head. "I won't tell you."

Tears stung her eyes. She was so close after ten years. So close that it was within reach. "Why not?"

"Because the truth is leverage. Leverage over everyone and everything in this town. Leverage is power. Do you know what you can get people to do if you know their secrets?"

Bethany bit back a sob, determined to keep her weakness hidden. While she had been baiting Damien, he had been prodding her for her weaknesses. She wasn't going to give him the satisfaction of proving him right.

"You have thirty seconds to get out of here," Kirk said, a dangerous edge to his tone. "Don't make me ask you again."

"Fine. I'll go," Damien muttered. "Just remember, I'm on to you now. So you had both better watch your backs."

"We're on to you, too," Kirk fired back.

Damien scowled as he moved away. Then he turned around and marched out of the apartment complex. The moment Damien disappeared into the shadows, Bethany collapsed against Kirk.

He wrapped his strong arm around her, propping her up so that she didn't fall. "Bethany—"

"Take me inside," she begged, clinging to his jacket. "Please."

With a grim nod, he steered her across the parking lot and headed into the apartment building.

As they entered her apartment, she let him guide her into the living room and help her sit down on the sofa. A lifetime of pain washed over her. They had been so close to the truth. So close to knowing if her father was innocent or guilty.

She had risked her relationship with Kirk to solve the mystery, and now she realized that she probably wasn't going to have either by the end of the night. Not Kirk and not the truth. Somehow, the thought of losing Kirk was so painful that she felt like she was being torn apart from the inside.

Tears started to fall and she wrapped her arms around herself. "I'm sorry," she gasped out as her vision blurred.

Kirk said nothing. Just sat down beside her and placed a gentle hand on her shaking shoulder. "He's gone now, Bethany. Damien can't hurt you."

"But I hurt you." She sucked in a shaky breath. "I went off on some phony date with him. It wasn't part of the plan. I was so desperate to get the truth that I hurt you." Frustrated with herself, she brushed her tears aside and turned to face him. "I swore I'd never lie to you, and I'll always keep that promise. Nothing happened between me and Damien. I only agreed to go out with him to get my foot in the door. That's it. Though, I don't expect you to forgive me."

"You're not in any position to expect anything from me," he said bitterly. "After what you did tonight..." He grimaced. "Damn, Bethany. I've always liked how bold you are. I've even made excuses for how impulsive you can be. But sometimes you can be reckless. Too reckless."

"I'm sorry—"

"You're not the only person in this relationship," he said, cutting her off. "You're not the only person who wants answers here."

She bit her lip to keep it from trembling. "I was selfish. We had a plan and I ignored it."

"I was worried about you tonight," he said. "I thought that Damien might have hurt you when I realized you'd gone off with him."

"I didn't think he was as dangerous as your dad said." She sighed heavily. "I figured that the chief of police was a safe person to be around. Maybe that makes me naïve."

"You're bold, but you still want to believe in justice." He paused and gave her a hard stare. "Maybe your idea for revenge was the right way to go after all."

She gasped. "What are you saying?"

"I'm saying that maybe you were right to carry around some of that hate," he said in a low voice that made her uneasy. His green eyes narrowed so dangerously that her heart tightened in fear.

"You can't mean that."

"I do mean it," he said forcefully. "You heard what that bastard Damien said. There's literally a cabal of criminals pulling the strings at the bank and who knows where else. To the point where even the mayor doesn't want to get on Damien's bad side."

His words filled her with renewed dread. "The mayor said that?"

He nodded. "Based on the mayor's hesitance to face the police chief, and what Damien revealed tonight, we're obviously dealing with a conspiracy. This is bigger than our parents."

Realization hit her. "Maybe that's why the prosecutor was so quick to give my father a plea deal. A trial might have implicated a lot of people."

"At this point, we don't know if our parents orchestrated something unethical or if they're victims of it," he murmured. "Either way, we now know that the police chief is involved somehow, and that he answers to a shadowy group of people."

Hearing him lay it all out was chilling. "So, what do we do now?"

"The first thing I'm going to do tomorrow is start setting up a security system for your apartment," he said.

An argument was on the tip of her tongue, but he shot her a warning glance.

"Don't bother challenging me on this," he added. "I'm paying for it and that's final."

"What if my landlord doesn't approve?" she asked meekly.

"I don't care," he said firmly. "You're getting a security system whether you like it or not."

She let out a heavy sigh. As much as she liked her independence, it was nearly impossible to argue with him now. Making an enemy of a police chief who answered to crooks was going to put her in a dangerous position. Better to be safe than sorry, even if she was uneasy about Kirk paying. "Okay. I can't argue with that."

"In the meantime, I'll be staying over tonight to make sure you're safe," he said.

Relief washed over her so suddenly that she clutched her chest. "You mean you're not...you're not ending things between us?"

Reaching for her hand he shook his head vigorously. "No. Of course not. You're not getting rid of me, Bethany, I promise you."

"You're still angry, though. I can sense it."

His jaw clenched. "It's probably best if I sleep on the couch tonight," he said, all but confirming her suspicions. If he wanted to sleep separately he was definitely still angry, and she didn't blame him one bit.

"I understand." She pulled her hand back and rose. "Wait here."

Kirk's brow furrowed in confusion, but he didn't say anything to stop her as she dashed to her bedroom.

Heart racing, she opened her nightstand drawer. He'd called her his girlfriend. Despite his hurt and anger, he still wanted to make this work. He had promised not to walk away this time, and though she had believed him, part of her worried. Worried that he would realize how much of a mess her life was and bail. But he hadn't done that tonight. Though he was obviously angry, he wanted to make this work. Wanted to make *them* work.

With a shaking hand, she retrieved the small bit of metal from the drawer and headed back into the living room. She resumed her seat beside him and took a deep, calming breath. "I've wanted to give this to you for a while now. I just didn't know if you'd want it."

"What is it?" he asked, very curious.

She took his hand and placed the cold metal in his palm. As terrifying as tonight had been, Bethany knew that it was time for her to fully commit to her feelings for him.

Chapter 12

She placed something hard and cool in his hand.

Kirk stared down, the small key shining in his hand. "Bethany, what's this?"

"It's the key to my apartment," she said softly. So softly he wasn't sure she'd actually said it.

"You're giving this to me?" he asked.

"Yes," she said with a nod. "It's the spare key my dad gave back to me when he moved out. I want you to have it."

He stared at the key for a long moment. A million thoughts raced through his head. Something like this was a big step. She was opening her apartment to him. Opening her heart. And her life. "This is..." His chest tightened with an emotion he'd never felt before in his life. It was filled with tenderness and a blazing passion all at the same time. A longing rose in his chest. An aching longing for her that made it hard to breathe. Somewhere underneath that ache was a sense that, for the first time in his life, he had truly found his home. A home, here in this apartment with Bethany.

"You don't have to accept it if you don't want to," she said suddenly, her voice trembling with trepidation. "It's a big step, and you're rightfully still mad at me—"

His free hand lifted to silence her, his fingers pressing against her full lips. "I'm accepting it."

A blush rose in her cheeks and she smiled, her lips curving against his fingers.

Kirk gazed at her for another lingering moment, mesmerized by how easily she controlled his heart. He had a mansion by the sea, yet this small apartment felt more like a home than anywhere ever had. As long as she was here, there was nowhere else he'd rather be.

She got up, trying to suppress a yawn as she stood. "I think it's time we go to bed. I'll go change out of my dress. You can take my bed and I'll take the couch."

"You have that backwards," he said. "You'll sleep in your bed and I'll take the couch."

"You're a guest. I can't let you sleep on the couch," she insisted.

He'd never be able to call himself a man if he drove her from her bed. Unwilling to entertain an argument he lay down on the sofa, stretching his legs out. "Goodnight, Bethany."

"But you're a guest," she repeated.

"You gave me a key, so I'm kind of more than a guest now." He shut his eyes.

"There's no arguing with you, is there?" she murmured.

Suddenly, he felt the warmth of her lips on his. His eyes snapped open. Having her soft, sinful mouth on his made him groan and close his eyes again to enjoy it. He was tempted to take her to bed, but tonight had been way too harrowing for her. A kiss would have to be enough. For now.

She pulled back and gave him a faint smile. "Goodnight, Kirk."

With that she padded into her bedroom, leaving him behind to fall asleep and dream about her all night long.

———◉———

HE TURNED THE KEY OVER in his hand, toying with it for the hundredth time this morning.

"Uh, Mr. Sterling?" His assistant, Camille, frowned from her seat across from him. "Would you like me to repeat the details of next week's schedule? I want to make sure that you heard everything."

"What?" He tore his eyes away from the key in his hand and glanced over at his assistant. "Could you go over that one more time? I missed some of that."

Camille tapped on the table impatiently and began reading from her planner again.

The minute she started speaking, his mind went back to what had been distracting him all day. Bethany. After spending the night at her place, they'd had a quick breakfast together and then he'd gone back to the mansion to get ready for work.

It was nearly lunch time now, and he had spent most of the day going over last night's events. Especially the moment she had given him the key to her apartment. As small as the gesture might seem, he knew that it was a big step. Big enough for him to still be obsessing over it when he should have been coming up with a way to fight Damien Kemp. That was how impossible it was for him to stop thinking about Bethany. Not even a confrontation with the city's chief of police could get him to stop thinking about his girlfriend.

Even though he loved his job, right now he had to fight the urge to skip work and go see her.

"Now that I'm done with the schedule, here's today's newspaper," Camille said, interrupting his thoughts. "You were mentioned in the social section."

Kirk took the newspaper from Camille and flipped to the social section. There was a photo of him talking to Mayor Howard above an article about last night's successful fundraiser. His eyes scanned the article. He'd been mentioned as a guest and a donor, but luckily nothing particularly salacious had been brought up. Considering some of the rumors he'd dealt with, this was thankfully tame and accurate.

He glanced at the photo one more time and noticed the police chief in the background. Seeing Damien again made his blood boil. Damien Kemp might look like the protector of the city, but after last night Kirk knew how dangerous the man was. If he could practically confess his sins, he obviously thought he was untouchable.

There was a good chance that Kemp was at least partially responsible for Bethany's pain. And he had dangled information about her father in front of her, and then snatched it away. It was like he got some kind of sick pleasure out of making her beg for the truth.

Angry all over again, Kirk tossed the newspaper aside and got to his feet.

"Is the meeting over, sir?" Camille asked in surprise. "We still have to go over last week's financial reports."

"We'll talk about that later," he said. "Why don't you take an early lunch?"

With a nod, she took her cue and exited the meeting room.

The photo of Kemp in the newspaper was bringing back all of last night's anger. Bethany might have put her anger and bitterness behind her, but Kirk's rage had finally begun to flare. Someone was pulling the strings at his bank. He was the vice president, and he was being kept in the dark about what was really going on. Letting this continue was no longer an option.

He grabbed his stuff and headed out of the meeting room. Maybe he couldn't look through the illegal things that Damien Kemp was doing, but he still had access to the legal things. There was bound to be a weakness there, and Kirk intended to exploit it.

Once he got to his office, he booted up his computer and started sleuthing. Bethany might be satisfied with the truth, but that was no longer enough for him.

"BETHANY, WE NEED TO talk." His voice was low, like he was trying to make sure nobody would overhear him over the phone.

She glanced around the well-lit room, making sure that nobody in the waiting area was listening in. Her heart clenched as anxiety poured over her. Maybe he hadn't forgiven her for last night. Maybe he was having second thoughts about their relationship. "Is everything okay?"

"I think I've found something about Damien Kemp," he said.

Bethany almost breathed a sigh of relief at that. Even though the police chief scared her, the thought of losing Kirk scared her far more. "What is it? What did you find?"

"Not over the phone," he said. "Are you free in an hour?"

"I'm about to go to a meeting with the director of the San Diego School of Creative Art and Design," she explained. "They might have an opportunity for me, but I'm not sure how long the meeting is supposed to last."

"Bethany, that's great! I hope the opportunity works out, especially since they're your alma mater," he said.

She smiled, grateful for his encouragement. Her years at the design school had been a haven from the craziness that came with her father going to prison. Now that the school had invited her to show off some of her designs at one of its frequent fashion shows, she was excited to be back. As a former student, she had been invited to take part in a fashion show. And though it wasn't something as glamorous as New York Fashion Week, the exposure would be good for her.

"I can meet you at the design school," he continued. "We can talk there. I doubt we'll have many reporters to fend off."

"Okay, sounds great. I'll call you as soon as my meeting is finished."

After her meeting with the director, she headed into one of the fast food restaurants on campus. She spotted Kirk at a corner table as she pushed through the late afternoon crowd. The smell of grease and ketchup was taking her back to her time as a student here. Everything about this place was so familiar that it felt like home. She had been just like these students once. Excited, exhausted, and riddled with anxiety about finances.

"I hope you haven't been waiting long." When she got to Kirk, she plopped down onto the chair across from him. Exhaustion after her long day of meetings and narrowing down commercial properties for her shop was getting to her.

"I've only been here for about fifteen minutes." He leaned forward to kiss her gently on the lips, making her stomach flutter.

"Kirk, what if someone sees us?" Despite her anxiety about them being seen, she couldn't keep from smiling.

"I don't think these students are going to notice us." He motioned to the crowd of students, all of them oblivious to their existence. "I hope you don't mind that I ordered you a cheeseburger and some fries." Kirk pushed a tray of food to her side of the table.

"Thanks." She popped a fry into her mouth, grateful for the food after working herself ragged all day. "I don't have long since I'm supposed to be meeting with some students in about forty-five minutes. I'm supposed to be mentoring them through this."

He smiled, his eyes lighting up with pride. "That's great. I'm proud of you."

She waved her hand dismissively. "It isn't like I'm being whisked off to a fashion show in Paris. This is just a small student project, so it isn't a big deal."

"Yeah, but you'll be helping a new generation of designers," he said. "Sounds like a big deal to me."

"Well, when you put it like that it does sound important." She gave him a small smile, grateful to have him and his support. Having someone get excited about her accomplishments—even the small ones—was something she hadn't experienced much since she was a kid. For years she had celebrated her little victories alone. Now, she had Kirk. And he believed in her so much that it renewed her excitement about her dreams. "So, what did you find out?"

The expression on his face turned serious and he leaned forward. "We didn't get a chance to get caught up after the fundraiser yesterday. Something the mayor said got me thinking about Damien Kemp's finances."

"He did mention that he lost money during the embezzlement scandal," she said, going over her conversation with the police chief in her mind.

He nodded. "The mayor said the exact same thing, so I did some digging at the office today. Damien Kemp's personal money came from that era, but he has another account at the bank."

"Lots of people have more than one account, though." She started to eat her burger.

"Yes, but this account is a shared account that's just... there."

She frowned, confused. "What do you mean?"

"I mean, I can't figure out when it was opened," he replied. "All I know is that the account existed during your father's time, as a savings account. Nobody was attached to it, until Damien was added to it *after* my parents took over the bank from your father. It's a shared account, but he's the only person connected to it."

"Do you think that's where he launders the money?" she asked.

"That's what I originally thought but the money is coming from inside the bank, not outside," he said. "Which means it's not getting laundered through this account. The strange thing is that, all through the embezzlement scandal, a lot of money did go through that account. It came from the bank itself, and so far looks legal, but it was way more than an average police officer's salary."

Her stomach twisted painfully. "If a lot of money went through that account, then maybe it was a way to secretly pay Damien off. Maybe someone kept the money there until Damien got access to it."

"That's what it looks like to me," he said with a nod. "Which means that the chief of police managed to get his hands on a lot of embezzled money. We're talking millions of dollars that went to this account and then just... disappeared."

"So that means Damien was benefitting from the embezzlement, or—"

"Or he was handing the money over to the criminals he answers to," Kirk finished for her.

Her eyes went wide with shock. "He'd need access to a senior staff member at the bank. And he did mention that he befriended my father. Maybe that's how he did it. Befriended my dad and manipulated him into asking for loans. Then somehow he got my father to repay the loans by putting the repayment in an account Damien managed to access years later. Which would make it a pretty clever plan. Not many people have that kind of patience when it comes to accessing a lot of money."

"My guess is that he and his shady business partners lured your dad into their scheme by giving him loans and then they squeezed him to repay with a ton of accumulated interest. Or they used the loans as some kind of blackmail. Either way, your father would have had to pay them back over time. I suspect these aren't the types of people who put up with late payments. They're basically thugs in suits, and if they've got cops on their payroll they wouldn't hesitate to resort to violence to get their money back. So, maybe your dad knew this, put some money into this account to satisfy these criminals that Damien worked for, and then years later, after the dust settled, Damien got the cash to his bosses."

"Meaning my father might have embezzled money to prevent these people from hurting him," she said. "So... he didn't steal that money for himself. He was trying to stop these people."

"That's just my theory," he said. "We'd need more proof. Besides, the theory doesn't explain the money laundering my dad mentioned, and it doesn't explain my parents' role in this."

"It's something, though," she said.

"Definitely. I don't think we would have gotten this far if you hadn't baited Damien the way you did last night," Kirk said. "Getting him to admit your father went to him for loans might end up being helpful for us."

She heard the hint of admiration in his voice. "Well, after speaking with him, I started to see he was the type of man who has an inferiority complex. He knows he has faults and, though he'll admit to them and maybe even joke about them, he hates having other people bring them up. His ego can't handle people thinking he isn't good enough. If I let him think I didn't believe he was capable of taking down my dad, then he'd get angry enough to want to prove that he actually could."

He grinned. "Who knew you knew so much about psychology?"

"A lot of it stuff I learned from my mother. She always said that people reveal themselves if you let them talk long enough."

He paused. "Any ideas on what we do now? We can't trick Damien the same way this time."

"Honestly, I've had such a long day," she said.

"Of course. You're exhausted, and you still have to meet with your students," he murmured. "We can talk about this later. In the meantime, I'll get in touch with your landlord so that I can set up a security system at your apartment as soon as possible."

"I won't be able to talk you out of being overprotective again, will I?"

"Nope. I'm going to take Damien very seriously whether you like it or not."

She slumped back in her seat with a sigh. "There really is no arguing with you when you're this determined."

"How about I call your landlord tomorrow, convince him, and then I can take you out of town on a weekend trip?"

Excitement made her sit up straight. "Oh, what romantic plans have you got in store for us?"

"I promise we won't be getting in a rowboat," he said with an apologetic smile. "All you need to know is that we're going to be wine tasting, and you should pack your bags for an overnight stay this weekend. There will be a pool, so if you want to swim pack a bathing suit. I'll book a place for us to stay overnight, and you'll have your own room... if you want to take this trip with me."

"That sounds like so much fun. I definitely want to go." Getting to spend more time with him despite their hectic schedules was what she wanted more than anything. And if they were going wine tasting, that was just an added bonus.

They soon finished eating, and Kirk walked with her all the way across the campus to one of the fashion design workrooms for her meeting.

Before she opened the workroom door to step inside, he took her hand. "Call me when you get home safely," he said.

"I will," she promised as she craned her neck to gaze up at him. They'd been out together in public more than once now, but it still thrilled her. Just holding his hand in public like this made her giddy. Pulse racing, she pressed her lips to his for a tender, lingering kiss.

He released her hand to gently grip her waist, making her feel safe and held. When he pulled back, he gently caressed her cheek and smiled at her. "I'm already looking forward to this weekend."

"So am I."

"Don't forget to call me." Kirk pressed another quick kiss to her lips and then headed back out the way they'd come.

She watched him walk away until he was out of sight, and she realized that giddy feeling hadn't gone away. Despite their argument the night before, he was still here. Still ready to make things work between them. There were still so many unknowns and so many mysteries they hadn't solved. But now she could dare to hope that he'd be by her side no matter how rocky the road ahead of them got.

Chapter 13

He picked her up in a flashy, vintage convertible.

Her mouth dropped open when she saw him step out of the silver car. Clutching her duffel bag tightly she gazed at him as he walked towards her, the picture of casual, masculine elegance. It was like he had just walked off the set of one of those old Italian movies.

Kirk was sporting a pair of designer sunglasses, his dark hair slicked back so stylishly she had to fight the urge to run her fingers through his hair. The rolled-up sleeves of his crisp white shirt revealed his muscular forearms.

When he reached her, Kirk gave her a dazzling smile and took the duffel bag from her.

"It's heavy," she warned him.

He shrugged. "Nothing I can't handle." The deep baritone of his voice had her stomach doing flips. Still smiling, he leaned closer to kiss her gently. "You look beautiful."

"Thank you." She'd made sure to wear a flirty sundress for the trip, and she blushed as he took off his sunglasses to gaze at her.

Letting out a soft, appreciative whistle, Kirk took her hand. "I'm the luckiest man in the world, aren't I?"

She laughed, loving the feel of her hand in his. "I'd say top three luckiest for sure."

He laughed and guided her across the parking lot to his car. After he set the heavy duffel bag in the back of the car with ease, he helped her into her seat and got behind the wheel.

"This is a gorgeous car," she told him.

"Gorgeous car for a gorgeous girl," he said as he revved the engine.

There were butterflies in her stomach as he pulled out of the parking lot and headed down the street. This was going to be their first weekend trip together, and she couldn't wait to see what he had in store for them.

She leaned back in her seat as the wind whipped at her hair. "So, I'm guessing this trip means you're taking a renewed interest in wine?"

"Yes, I am," he said. "Parts of upper-class culture don't appeal to me, but you've opened my eyes to appreciating some things. Like food and wine."

"Glad to hear it," she said.

"And, since I'm taking this car for a spin for the first time in ages, maybe it's a sign that I should take an interest in cars," he said. "Instead of thinking I'm above all the upper-class stuff, I need to remember how fortunate I am to have all this money."

She nodded. "That's the best way to think of it. It doesn't have to be about acquiring things to impress shallow people. It can be about enjoying so many wonderful things that life can offer."

"Well, I have you to thank for opening my eyes. When you talk about your childhood, you talk about your grandmother's orchard or riding horses. You used your privilege to have experiences and make memories. That's what I want. I don't have to let my job be the only thing that guides me, you know?"

Knowing that he was opening his heart more made her feel warm and happy inside. Even though their families were still dealing with their past mistakes and misdeeds, that didn't mean that they couldn't try to enjoy their lives now. They both deserved to step out of the shadow of their families and live a little.

They arrived at the Southern Valley Resort and Winery early in the afternoon. She stepped out of the car to take in the breathtaking landscape. The resort looked like a Mediterranean villa with its stucco walls and red-tile rooftop. Trees and rose bushes decorated the exterior, and to her right were the rolling hills of Southern California.

"Let's go check out our suite." He placed a firm hand on the small of her back, the touch burning through the paper-thin fabric of her dress.

As she walked with him to the front desk inside, she was blissfully aware of the weight of his hand on her back. With their accommodations worked out, they followed the bellhop across the property to their very own luxury bungalow.

The décor was rustic but chic, with the delightful scent of lavender in the air. Excited to see her room, she rushed across the living room and flung her bedroom door open. There was a huge bed covered in the fluffiest pillows, and a big screen TV taking up an entire wall. The adjoining bathroom was wall-to-wall polished marble. One night here had to cost a small fortune, and she knew arguing with Kirk about money would go nowhere. He really did seem determined to spoil her every way he could.

With her room explored, she stepped back out.

"Hey, Bethany, come check out this view," Kirk said.

She followed the sound of his distant voice until she found him on the terrace outside. The view of the landscape was spectacular. An expansive vineyard spread out and seemed to go on for miles. Beyond the vineyard were sloping green hills. Overhead, there wasn't a cloud in the bright blue sky.

Much closer to the terrace was an inviting aquamarine swimming pool that they seemed to have all to themselves.

"It's perfect," she said as she reached his side.

"I knew you'd like it," he said. "I heard about this place forever ago, but I'd never taken the time to come here. I'm glad I waited to share it with you." He wrapped his arm around her, pulling her close.

Loving the security of his hard, solid body, she snuggled against him. "I'm glad, too. When I was a kid my family would go down to my father's winery, but I was just a kid. My cousins and my brother and I spent most of those family trips hanging out by the pool. Now I get to experience this place in a whole different way."

"If you do want to swim, the private pool is all ours," he told her.

"I'll swim a little later," she said. "What did you have planned for this afternoon?"

"We're getting a guided tour of the vineyard," he said.

"That sounds like fun." She paused. "I hope none of the other guests on the tour recognize us."

He lowered his arm and took her hand in his. "No worries. This is a private tour. I've made sure this weekend is just about you and me. After all the craziness of the past couple of weeks, it will be just the two of us."

That was music to her ears.

———— ⬤ ————

AFTER THEY GOT SETTLED into their suite, Kirk led her out to the vineyard to meet their tour guide. With the introductions made their tour guide started to lead them around the vineyard, giving details on the finer points of cultivating grapes.

A lot of the details were lost on him since he was still a wine novice, but Bethany's entire face lit up as the tour guide led them down row after row of grape vines. There were workers tending to the leafy vines, some of them tipping their hats politely in greeting as they toured the fields.

Though he didn't pick up on everything their tour guide said, the tour was worth it just to see how happy it made Bethany. She asked many questions, her genuine curiosity infectious.

Getting out of the city for the weekend had been the right idea. Hostility between their families and Damien's connection to the whole shady business was putting a strain on both of them. Taking the time to be on their own together like this was going to help to take some of the pressure off. Just seeing her smile was already making the weight on his shoulders feel lighter.

"Now," the tour guide said once their tour of the vineyard was over, "how about a tour of the winery itself?"

Bethany nodded enthusiastically. "Yes, that sounds like fun."

"Wonderful. Follow me," he said.

As they followed after the tour guide, she took Kirk's hand and smiled. That smile that made her bright blue eyes light up—eyes so blue they rivaled the sky—did something indescribable to his heart.

There was an irresistible glow about her out here. Here, where she was in her element. As beautiful as their surroundings were, she was what stole his breath away. Her lush lips curved up into the most heart-stopping smile. And that dress she was wearing skimmed the curves of her body. A light breeze lifted her dress up just enough to show off her supple thighs. He was so mesmerized by her that he almost forgot about the tour entirely, until she tugged on his hand to lead him away.

The tour guide showed them into the main building of the winery, stopping to give them a demonstration of the grapes being pressed in sturdy metal presses. Finally, they stepped into the dim wine cellar, with Bethany excitedly chatting away about wine barrels. He could listen to her talk about the most mundane topics and never get tired of listening to her.

When they were finished touring the cellar, the tour guide headed back outside. "Now that today's tour is concluded, I would like to thank you both for being such wonderful guests," the tour guide said. "We have a whole range of events and activities, so don't think all the excitement ends with today's tour."

"Thank you so much for showing us around," she said. "We learned a lot today."

"My pleasure," the tour guide said with a smile. "If you decide to order room service this evening, you will get a complimentary bottle of red wine right from our winery. All you have to do is mention that you went on a tour with me. Tell them Jeremy said you could have a free bottle."

"Oh, that's so kind," she said. "Thank you again, Jeremy."

They got back to their bungalow as the sun started to set, casting a fiery orange glow across the sky.

"How about we watch the rest of the sunset before we order dinner?" she suggested.

"Sounds good to me," he said, heading for the terrace out back.

He pulled out a chair for her, and once she was sitting comfortably he took a seat beside her.

She sank back in the chair with a contented sigh, the hem of her dress sliding up again, revealing her thighs. "This is a great view, isn't it?"

"Yes," he said, barely able to get the word out.

Bethany turned to look at him, her eyes following his gaze to her exposed thighs. She laughed. "Kirk."

"Sorry. I—" He cringed. "I have a hard time paying attention to anything other than you."

Her cheeks turned rosy and she gave him a coy smile. "We can always go to your bedroom if you're so distracted."

He got to his feet the moment she got the words out and took her hands. "Bethany, I—"

A sultry laugh cut him off, and she stood up to kiss him. He pulled her close, his hands taking her waist, and held her soft body against him. Her mouth was soft, and so inviting that she welcomed him in as he slipped his tongue in to meet hers. Beneath his fingertips, he felt her quiver against his body. Desire coiled through him, radiating a burning need right down to his soul. As his grip on her tightened he deepened the kiss, tasting her as he let his tongue entwine with hers.

Her response to him was to slide her slender arms around his shoulders. Their bodies were pressed up together so closely that he could swear he felt her heartbeat. Her soft breasts crushed up against his chest, his desire for her turning into an aching arousal.

She broke the kiss, pulling back to gaze into his eyes. Her breasts heaved as she struggled to breathe. Fire burned in her eyes, turning them into blue flames. "Take me to your room."

Chapter 14

He didn't need to be told twice. Still holding on to her hips, he steered her into his bedroom and shut the door behind him.

She backed away towards the bed, her sensuous lips curving up into a shy smile. There was something so irresistibly pure about her. From her halo of golden hair to the sway of her hips as she moved, he would never get tired of watching her. Of seeing how her body would mesmerize him in ways he never thought possible.

When she stopped against the bed, she allowed herself to lie down on the bed, propping herself up on her elbows as she gazed up at him. She kicked her shoes off and suddenly, without any prompting, she spread her legs.

Hot damn. As she opened her legs, she hiked up her dress until he got an eyeful of her dangerously red panties. His heart slammed in his chest at the sight and he was aroused even more. Too achingly hard to do anything but stand frozen as he stared at the most wanton woman he had ever met in his life.

If he thought she was going to show him mercy, that thought was dashed when she reached up and tugged her panties off. A glimpse of her bare, glistening flesh made him want to drop to his knees and worship her.

"I'm waiting," she said, her voice a husky purr.

Swallowing hard, he moved closer to her and dropped down to his knees in front of her.

Her eyes went wide. "What are you—"

Kirk lifted his hand to silence her. "Let me taste you, Bethany." He hadn't tasted her in far too long. If he didn't have her now he would go crazy.

Eyes still on him, she gave him a wicked smile. The wicked, knowing smile of a temptress. Without saying anything, she spread her legs even wider for him. She bit her lip and then said, "Do whatever you want to me."

Giving her pleasure was his only goal. Hearing the desperate plea in her voice, he planted his hands firmly on her knees and lowered his mouth to the most secret part of her. Her sweet wetness was the most divine thing he had ever tasted. Burying his face between her legs, he flicked his tongue across her slick heat.

With a moan, Bethany arched her back. "*Yes.*"

He swirled his tongue into her, working her into a frenzy as she gasped for breath. His grip on her knees tightened as he licked at her furiously, tasting her essence like he would die if he didn't.

Suddenly, he felt her run her hand through his hair. He stopped to look up at her and found that the fire in her eyes was on the verge of burning out of control. In her eyes, he saw that she wanted more. And he was going to give her exactly what she wanted.

Her face was flushed, her hair now a tangled mess. Seeing her like this excited him. Let him know that he had put that excited look on her face. He was the one who had her panting for more.

Kirk pulled back and stood up, quickly undoing the buttons of his shirt. As she watched him undress she licked her lips, her body trembling as he took his clothes off. Finally, he stripped away his boxer briefs and stood naked in front of her.

Her eyes locked on his and she shifted on the bed to take off her dress. When she tossed the thin fabric aside, he realized she wasn't wearing a bra underneath. She was now totally naked, her bare flesh an invitation to lose himself in her. The sight of her pink nipples nearly made him groan out loud.

She climbed further up the bed and lay down on her back.

Seeing her perfect body sprawled out on his bed for him nearly drove him insane. She was beautiful. Her body absolutely perfect, with curves that tempted him beyond reason. Every inch of her creamy skin made his mouth water. Turned his thoughts into a haze of raw need.

Those mesmerizing blue eyes of hers lowered to take in his manhood, and she licked her lips again. Without a sound she beckoned to him. He got onto the bed with her and lowered himself down on her.

"Are you ready for me?" he asked her.

In response, she wrapped her legs around his waist, locking him in place. "Always."

Desperate to be inside her, he thrust into her tight wetness. She clenched around him and he was drowning in pleasure. It gripped him so tightly, it knocked the air out of him. His eyes met hers and he started to rock into her, giving her everything he had.

A moan tore from her throat and she raised her hips to meet his hard strokes. He thrust deeper and deeper into her, ecstasy shooting through his body. They didn't need words when they had this. Not when he knew the intensity of her desire as her nails dug into his back. Her cries were so loud they shut out every coherent thought in his head. All he had now was feeling. All he wanted to give her was more pleasure than she could stand.

She writhed beneath him, moaning his name. He sped up the pace of his thrusts, fast losing control as ecstasy seized him. No other woman had ever made him lose control like this. With her, he didn't hold back. Didn't hide. When he was with her he gave himself over completely, and he knew she did the same. Knew because her legs gripped him tighter as she clenched around him again, milking him until he was nearly spent.

More pleasure slammed through him, pushing him to the edge of release. With one last powerful thrust into her he felt her spasm around him, a loud moan signaling her climax. At the sound of her release, he came so hard and fast that he collapsed.

As he tried to roll away from her to ease the weight on her body she held him fast, refusing to let go. He felt her chest heave as she sucked in ragged breaths. Finally, she eased her grip on him, letting him pull away and lie on his back.

His heart thudded in his chest and he inhaled deeply, trying to catch his breath. With his breathing slowing down a fraction, Kirk reached for her and held her tightly to him. He glanced at her to see how she was, and he found that her eyes were closed, her breaths even. Talking to her would have to wait, because she had fallen fast asleep in his arms. Not that he minded. If he could stay in his bed with her forever, he would gladly do it. The outside world was nothing compared to her.

BETHANY WOKE UP TO the sound of him wheeling a room service trolley laden with silver platters into the living room outside the bedroom door. She yawned and stretched. After having amazing sex with him, she'd had such a good nap that she hadn't felt this well rested in ages.

"I ordered food for us," Kirk said. "I figured you'd be hungry when you woke up."

"It smells heavenly," she said. "Hang on, I'm going to go freshen up." Wrapping the sheet around her, she scurried out of his bedroom and into hers. She grabbed her duffel bag and went into the bathroom to get cleaned up and put on one of the comfortable resort bathrobes.

When she headed back out, she found him uncorking the bottle of red wine.

"This is the wine the tour guide gave us. I thought we could have dinner out on the terrace," he said.

"I can't wait to try the wine," she said excitedly. Knowing that the wine was made right here on the property made it extra special.

She followed him as he wheeled the trolley outside, the cool night air refreshing her. While he started to pile their plates with food, she poured two glasses of wine.

The distant sound of her cell phone ringing caught her attention so she set the glasses down and rushed into her bedroom to answer it. She wasn't expecting anyone to call, though if it was Jane wanting to talk about the shop or Naya wanting to shoot the breeze she could always ask them to call back later. All she wanted to do tonight was to relax and spend time with Kirk.

She grabbed her phone from the nightstand, frowning when she realized that no number came up. "Hello?" she said.

All she heard was silence. Must be a bad connection.

"Hello? Can you hear me?" she asked.

The line crackled and then came the sound of heavy, insistent breathing. An icy claw of fear gripped her heart as she realized that the breathing was deliberate. "Who is this?" she asked, unable to keep her voice from shaking.

Her stomach lurched as the breathing grew louder, more menacing. It wasn't the sound of someone who was out of breath. This was deliberate. Hard inhales, followed by the forced exhale of a predator. Even without words, she knew the sound was a warning. No. A threat.

"Please leave me alone," she cried. "Don't call me ever again."

Mocking laughter filled her ears, and then the line went dead.

Icy, oily dread crept down her spine, making her shiver. Her mouth went dry, her throat so clogged up she couldn't call out for Kirk. Couldn't call out to the one person who had always made her feel safe. Struggling to catch her breath, she stumbled into the living room and then out onto the terrace.

Kirk jumped from his seat. "Is everything okay? You look like you've seen a ghost."

Her heart raced as she played the sound of that evil laugh in her mind again. Never had she heard such cruelty in one sound. "Someone called me," she choked out. "All I heard was breathing on the other end. And then they laughed. Evil laughter. Like a crazy person."

"What the hell?" He stepped over to her and curled his fingers around her shoulders. "Do you know who it was? Was there a number?"

She shook her head. "No. There wasn't a number. I know it sounds like nothing, but it was the creepiest thing I've ever heard."

"I believe it," he said grimly. "I can see it on your face."

A shudder made her wrap her arms around him. Only Kirk could force her heart to stop racing like it would never slow down again. "Kirk, I think it was—"

"Damien Kemp," he finished for her. "That bastard."

"How on earth did he get my number?" She shuddered again, knowing that she'd have to change her number if she wanted to stay safe. There was no telling what else the police chief might do with that kind of information.

"I don't know. I'm going to call resort security," he said.

She let go of him, allowing him to stalk back into their suite. More dread propelled her to follow after him. The thought of being alone even for a moment was unbearable.

Kirk grabbed the phone on the coffee table. "I doubt Kemp is out here, but it's best to tell security about this just in case."

He'd barely gotten the words out when the ear-splitting sound of shattering glass filled the room.

Bethany whirled around to find that shards of glass at her feet, a brick less than a yard away. "Kirk!" Her gaze lifted to the sight of one of the back windows smashed in, a curtain fluttering in the breeze that was rushing in through the broken window.

"Who the hell's out here?" Kirk rushed by her until he was back on the terrace.

"No one." Seeing him run towards the danger terrified her. The thought of him being hurt was too much to bear. "Come back inside. Please."

"I know you're hiding out here!" He stalked out of sight, heading into the shadows.

"No. Kirk, no." Pushing her fears aside, she raced out onto the terrace to follow after him. She refused to let him face the danger alone.

Nobody was out on the terrace. Kirk just vanished into the darkness that extended beyond the lights outside. Clutching her robe, she headed into the shadows.

Her eyes hadn't adjusted to the darkness so she stretched out her free hand, hoping to grip onto something that might steady her. "Kirk."

All she could hear was the night song of crickets and the faint sound of laughter from a nearby suite. Her heart thudded in her chest. What if Kirk had been attacked? Or worse?

Panic made her plunge further and further into the inky blackness. Suddenly someone gripped her arms from behind, dragging her back. Adrenaline rushed through her and she struggled to free herself. She wouldn't let this unknown attacker take her away. Not when Kirk needed her to find him.

She shrieked in terror as the attacker's grip on her tightened.

"Bethany, it's me." Kirk's voice. "It's me. I'm not going to hurt you."

Relief forced a sob from her, and the moment his grip loosened she turned around and collapsed against him. Hot tears stung her eyes and started to slide down her cheeks. "I thought..." She gasped for breath through her sobs.

"It's me," he reassured her. "I didn't find whoever threw that brick."

"I thought you'd been hurt," she forced out.

He held her tightly, the strength of his arms adding to her relief. "I'm fine. We need to go back inside and alert resort security."

Exhausted from her terror, she let him guide her out of the darkness and back inside their suite. She stepped gingerly around the broken glass on the living room floor to sink down onto the sofa. Fear overwhelmed her so much she barely heard him make the call to security. Barely noticed when a security guard showed up minutes later to patrol the terrace outside. When a resort maid showed up to clean up the glass, she got up to help the her pick up the sharp pieces. So did Kirk. Somehow she knew that neither of them wanted anyone to have to deal with the terror on their own. It wasn't the maid's fault that a maniac was after them.

When the maid finally left, Bethany sat on the sofa again. Kirk sat beside her, holding her close.

"How did he know we were out here?" she asked, her voice a shaky whisper.

"He's the chief of police. He must have his ways."

"We can't stay here," she said.

"It's too late to leave now," he murmured, "but we'll head out first thing in the morning, I promise."

The thought of spending the night in this tranquil place had filled her with excitement earlier, but that was gone now. All she wanted to do was get as far away from the police chief as possible. They had made a very dangerous enemy, and she was terrified of what he would do next.

"What do we do now?" Sleep wasn't going to be an option tonight. She was too on edge to even think about sleeping.

"We need to hit back at Damien," he said, pulling away from her.

"Hit back?" She shook her head vigorously. "No. He's one of the most powerful men in San Diego. Not only does he have the entire police force behind him, but he also has ties to shady people. We tried getting the truth out of him and we got something. Pushing him now will only make it worse."

His jaw clenched. "The truth isn't enough. This man is responsible for your family's misfortune. Maybe your dad stole all that money, but he went to prison. Kemp has never had to pay for what he's done."

"We don't have proof," she insisted. "Even if we wanted to go after him, what would we do? We can't go to the police. Your money can't get us out of this, Kirk. Stopping the chief of police is the one thing money cannot buy."

"No, I refuse to accept that. I'm not letting Kemp get away with this. At the very least he should pay for threatening us tonight." Kirk got out of the living room and returned a minute later with his laptop in hand.

She frowned. "What are you doing?"

"I have to confront Kemp," he said harshly as he resumed his seat.

"You're going to publicly confront him?" Panic tugged at her stomach. "That could make this worse."

Ignoring her warning, Kirk booted up his computer and started typing furiously. "There's got to be another event I can get into. If he's forced to acknowledge what he's done in public, maybe he'll lose some of his power."

"Or maybe he'll shrug it off and come after you with something dangerous."

"He's going to be at a fine arts auction this week. Most of the stuff is priceless art or ancient artifacts," Kirk said. "I can go. Show him that I'm not afraid of him."

"He seems to have a thing for art." She glanced at him. "Do you really think this is the kind of place you want to confront him in? Think of the kinds of people who go to auctions like that. They could be potential clients. Do you really want to risk the bank's reputation?"

"Art..." He set his laptop on the coffee table. "Bethany, you're brilliant."

"Wait—"

"Art! That's it. That's how Kemp launders the money. Why didn't I see it before?" Kirk stood up. "Plus, this art collection has been in storage for ten years. That has to be where all that money went. The money your father was accused of embezzling might be at an auction house right now."

Her mouth fell open. Never in a million years had she ever thought the truth would lead to something like this. "You think that's how the money got funneled out of the bank? How the police chief gets the money to his superiors?"

"Yes. His superiors make shady deals, and he uses the money to buy art. He probably sells the art back for a profit and gets the money back to his bosses."

"And if he wanted to get the money out of the bank, he'd do the same thing," she murmured. "Buy the art. Then resell it for a profit and give it to his bosses."

"While he gets a cut of it," Kirk said.

"Damn." It made total sense, and yet guessing the truth actually made things more dangerous. The police chief had allies and enemies too terrified to resist him throughout the city. Not only in the local government and police force, but in elite circles as well. Even with Kirk's wealth and privilege, that was a tough thing to counter. "Even if we got proof, he'd see us coming. We can't confront him now. That would just give him an even bigger head-start than he has now."

"Not if we stop him now." Kirk's brow furrowed as he started to think. "Okay, if we can't stop him, maybe his bosses can."

"You mean the criminals he works for?" She frowned. "How would we even convince them to do that?"

"Make them angry. Force them to come after the police chief. Think about it... if they think that Kemp betrayed them somehow, they'll finish him," he answered. "Plus, we'll finally make someone pay for all the pain you've been through."

Now that Kirk had thawed her icy heart, revenge just didn't mean all that much to her. "I don't know. It's dangerous."

"This our way of getting the truth," he said. "Our parents have been too afraid of this guy to give us the truth. If he's dealt with, they might finally tell us what really happened."

She hadn't thought of that. If Damien Kemp was as dangerous as the mayor and Kirk's father had let on, getting him out of the way might be the best move. "We'll only have a few days to pull this off."

"I've got enough money at my disposal to be allowed into the auction," he said. "If we can pressure Damien into handing over the millions he's stolen, his superiors will have no choice but to come after him."

The idea was crazy. Not to mention risky. Bethany glanced at the broken window. Shattered by someone who had tried to hurt them. She had been through a lifetime of hurt.

"Okay." She took a deep breath. "I'm in."

"Good. We can get to work coming up with a plan tonight."

Her heart started to race at the prospect of what they were about to do. "Wait. I haven't explained my terms yet."

"Terms?" He gave her a questioning look.

Knowing that he was so willing to risk everything for her scared her to death. But she still steeled her spine. She wasn't going to let him face this alone. And she certainly wasn't going to let him do anything reckless. "This can't be about hurting Damien. Or about forcing the truth out of him. We've spent too much time focused on our own pain. Focused on selfish things like revenge or the truth. We should have been focusing on something else all along."

"What should we have been focused on?"

She raised her chin, determined. "Justice."

Chapter 15

He had to beg her to spend the next few days at his mansion. Sending her to her apartment alone was out of the question. Not while Damien Kemp was out there watching them. Plotting against them. The security system hadn't been installed at her apartment yet and he wasn't taking any chances. At least he had gotten her landlord to agree to setting up a security system.

As the day of the auction approached, he made sure to get a pass into the event. With that sorted out, he spent the next few days going over the plan with Bethany.

When the day of the auction came, he could sense her anxiety as they got ready.

Taking her hand before they got into his car, he said, "Don't worry. I'm here. We've got this."

She nodded and gave him a faltering smile. "Right."

Despite her obvious trepidation, she was facing this with him. Kirk admired her courage so much. He had never met anyone as brave as her, and he wasn't going to let her down. They were going to stop the man who had tormented their families. Stop him and bring him down.

When they got into the auction house Kirk gripped his laptop bag, scanning the place until he spotted Damien Kemp. The police chief was standing in the corner, surveying everything like he owned the place. Considering his shady dealings, he probably did have some kind of ownership over it all.

"I'll go get our seats," Bethany said to him.

Good. She was sticking to their plan.

He nodded and gave her hand one final reassuring squeeze. As she found seats for them, he crossed the room and approached the police chief.

Momentary shock flashed in Damien's eyes. "Sterling... what the hell are you doing here?"

"Surprised to see me after you attacked us this weekend?" Kirk bit out.

The auctioneer at the front podium started to speak, announcing the start of the auction. There was no turning back now. Kirk let his eyes fall on Bethany, who was working on their fallback plan in case something went wrong with the police chief. She'd bid on some of the pieces. Drive the price up. If she won the pieces, they'd resell them. And make a ton of money in the process.

Damien's eyes darted around the room. "Not here." He turned and walked through a door marked 'Staff Only'.

Kirk followed after him until Damien stopped at an office door with frosted glass and headed inside.

He didn't know if the police chief was stalling for time, but Damien was obviously rattled.

"Why are you here?" Damien said with a snarl as he sat at the desk.

"I know what you're doing," Kirk said. "This is how you launder the money."

Damien's eyes widened. "Who the hell told you that?"

"Who told you where I'd be this weekend?" Kirk shot back.

"Your chatty assistant told me last week," Damien said. "After I told her what lying to the chief of police would get her."

"You threatened Camille?" Kirk took an angry step towards the desk. "So you drove all the way down to wine country to get to us this weekend? Is that it?"

"Please. Don't insult me. I have associates to do that sort of work for me." Damien's eyes narrowed. "You need to leave. Now."

"Why? You scared that I figured out your scam?"

"I'm warning you, Sterling."

"You've got no cards left to play here, Damien," he stated. "I'm not leaving."

"Like hell you won't. I should call security," Damien said harshly.

"You won't. Because I know enough to bring the press down here. Maybe they won't be able to stop you, but you would never risk that kind of exposure. Not with the people you work with," Kirk muttered.

"The people I work with are dangerous people," Damien warned. "They're organized criminals. Mafia types. Drug dealers. These aren't the types of people you want to piss off."

"I know you don't want to piss them off," Kirk said. "Even though you're the police chief, you're still expendable. They'll cut you loose if they think the press will get wind of their crimes."

"We've got to be able to work something out," Damien said, lowering his voice. "What do you want? Are you strapped for cash?"

Kirk stared at him in disgust. "I'd bet you've never faced anyone who didn't have a price."

Damien started to shake visibly. "You want money, don't you? I can give you some."

"How about the money you took from Lloyd Livingston ten years ago?"

Damien swallowed hard. "Why are you so obsessed with the Livingston case?"

"You ruined the man's family. Ruined his children. Maybe Lloyd deserved to go to prison. But so did you, Damien. So did you." Knowing that Bethany had suffered so much anguish while Damien Kemp had been able to skirt by and rise up the ranks filled him with rage. The injustice was intolerable.

"I can't give you that money back," Damien said. "That's impossible. It's a ridiculous amount. There's got to be a more reasonable amount of money to keep you quiet."

"I know that what you're selling is connected to the Livingston case. Give me the money you're going to make from this auction and I'll give you a head-start," Kirk growled. "A head-start to get out of town before your bosses come after you."

"The auction has already started," he said desperately. "I need to re-sell these pieces if I have any hope of staying alive. My bosses will come after me if I don't get them that money."

"I'm giving you a head-start," Kirk repeated. "Besides, they might forgive a financial discrepancy enough to stick to merely breaking your legs. But they'll never forgive the truth leaking to the press. Revealing their existence and what they do isn't something you'll be able to survive, Damien. They will bury you out in the desert and you know it. Choose wisely. Money or your life."

Damien buried his head in his hands and groaned. "Fine."

Kirk pulled his laptop out of the bag. "The minute this auction ends, you're going to transfer the money into Bethany's account. I know you have the power to do that. You're going to make up for all her years of pain and suffering."

"You're both worse than your parents," Damien spat out.

So be it. As long as Bethany got the justice that was owed to her, Kirk didn't give a damn what the corrupt police chief thought.

He leaned against the door and locked it. Now, they would wait.

Minutes ticked by until an hour rolled around. An hour filled with a silence so tense that Kirk started to break out in an anxious sweat. Fear wasn't something he usually felt, and even with the upper hand he wasn't going to rest easy until the money was transferred.

Finally the auctioneer's voice boomed into a microphone, signaling the end of the auction.

"Transfer the money," Kirk said. "Now."

Hands shaking, Damien reached for the laptop. Kirk watched him like a hawk. Watched him transfer hundreds of millions of dollars into Bethany's new account at Sterling Investment Bank.

With the deed done, Kirk grabbed the laptop from him. "Good luck, Damien. You'll need it."

"So will you, Sterling," Damien retorted. "You think this is the end?" He laughed manically. "I might have to skip town, but I'll always be watching you. Always."

It was the last threat of a desperate man. Kirk sauntered out of the office without responding. When he found Bethany outside he wrapped his arms around her. "We did it."

"We did?" She broke apart from him to look into his eyes. "We did. Thank you, Kirk."

He gazed at her. Took in the gratitude that made her lips curve into a tiny, grateful smile. "You know you can always use this money to invest in your shop. That way you won't be forced to repay your investor, and you'll have more money than you ever dreamed of to pour into your dreams."

"No." She shook her head, eyes glistening. "I want to help all those people who lost so much. This is their money. We have to do the right thing and try to make their lives whole again. Think of all the charities that lost their donations. The people who lost their pensions and life savings. People who never got to go to college. The suicide victims who lost their lives because of cowardice and greed. Their loved ones deserve compensation. This needs to be made right."

Somehow, he knew that was exactly what she would say. She wouldn't be the woman he cared for if she hadn't. He put his arm around her shoulder and walked with her to his car. "That's the best thing to do. And I'll get right on it. By the end of the week, we'll have a foundation set up for all those people, and they'll finally get some justice."

THE NEXT DAY, KIRK took time from work to meet with his lawyer. Bethany had already filled out the documents needed to set up a foundation, and now Kirk was filling in the rest of it.

"I take it you want to remain anonymous?" his lawyer said from across the conference table.

Kirk nodded. "I don't want these people to be put through another media frenzy. Best to keep this to ourselves, while they start to pick up the pieces of their lives."

His lawyer nodded. "It will take time to disperse the funds, but we can set up the foundation pretty quickly."

"That's fine. I'll pay the taxes," Kirk said. "After my family's role in all this, it's the least I can do."

"Great. I'll be in touch." He lawyer took up the documents, said his goodbyes, and left.

It was hard to believe that a lot of this was over. While he still didn't know exactly what his parents had done, thousands of people were going to get what was owed to them. Maybe now the victims of the embezzlement would get a chance to heal.

Leaning back in the leather chair, Kirk grabbed the TV remote from the conference table and turned the TV on. There was a good chance that there would be news about Kemp on the local news. He flipped through the channels to one of the local stations, stopping on a news anchor reading a breaking news bulletin.

"We have multiple news stories breaking this hour, so let's get right to it," the anchor said, her face serious. "Earlier today, Police Chief Damien Kemp stepped down from his position in a surprise move that blindsided city officials. In an even more shocking turn of events, Mr. Kemp has reportedly left the San Diego area and his whereabouts are unknown at this time."

Gratitude and relief hit him. They wouldn't have to deal with the police chief anymore. Damien Kemp couldn't use the police force against them. It was the best news he'd heard in a long time, and he couldn't wait to get off work and celebrate with Bethany later tonight.

Kirk was about to turn off the television, when the anchor switched to the next story.

"And, in more shocking news today, well-regarded banking tycoon Bruno Sterling was arrested at his home just hours ago. Police officers raided his mansion," the anchorwoman said. Kirk's heart sank as images of his father being led away in handcuffs flashed on the screen.

"In addition to Mr. Sterling, his wife, Vivian Sterling, was also arrested as she stepped off her private jet today," the anchorwoman went on. "Charges have also been brought against their alleged co-conspirator, Lloyd Livingston, who has only recently been out on parole after a ten-year stint in prison for an embezzlement scheme that shocked the financial world. Though police haven't revealed exactly what the charges are sources close to the investigation have stated that they are incredibly serious, and more charges will be forthcoming."

He couldn't believe what he was seeing. His parents had been arrested and nobody had informed him. Nobody had warned him that this was coming.

Stunned, Kirk headed out of the conference room and rushed towards the elevator. Bethany was going to need him. Nobody had warned her the first time her father was arrested, and nobody had warned her now. This would absolutely shatter her.

Finally, he made his way to the parking lot and got into his black Mercedes. He had to see her. She was the only person who would understand this shock and agony. Despite the strained relationship he'd had with his parents lately, seeing footage of them being hauled off wounded him deeply. What had happened? What had they been accused of? Had their years of working with shady criminals finally come back to haunt them?

Desperate for answers, he stepped on the gas and raced towards Bethany's apartment. He knew that she'd been there all day working on some designs. If she hadn't heard the news, he was going to have to break it to her. Nothing could be more painful for her than finding out from the local news on TV.

When he arrived at her apartment, he jumped out of the car and ran. He grabbed the key she had given him from his pocket. Kirk didn't have the patience to wait for her to open the door for him. What he needed was Bethany in his arms. Now.

He froze when he got to her apartment door. It was wide open. Still holding the precious key in his hand, he walked inside. The apartment was completely torn apart. Ransacked. Sofas had been ripped open. Light bulbs smashed. Torn fabric strewed across the floor. The TV and the furniture inside had been turned over and damaged.

His heart slammed in his chest. "*Bethany.*" If she'd been hurt...

Pushing that gut-churning thought aside, Kirk started to search through the ransacked rooms until he found her in the kitchen.

Sprawled out on the kitchen floor. Face white. Her golden hair messily fanning around her. He moved closer to her and dropped down to his knees beside her, anguish tearing his insides to shreds.

"Bethany. Sweetie."

Her ashen skin was cold to the touch. Desperate to revive her, he lifted her head and saw the gash in her forehead. Blood ran down the side of her head into her hair. Her pale face was still. Her limbs at impossible angles. She looked broken. As broken as his own heart was now.

"Bethany, wake up. Please." He shook her insistently, over and over, begging her to open her eyes.

THE END... *for now*

Billionaire Banker Series

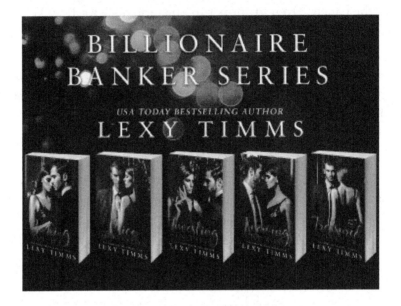

Book 1 – Banking on Him
Book 2 – Price of Passion
Book 3 – Investing in Love
Book 4 – Knowing Your Worth
Book 5 – Treasured Forever

Knowing Your Worth Blurb

KIRK STERLING HASN'T seen Bethany Walker since the day he dumped her. He broke up with her to protect her from his powerful family, but he hasn't gotten over her. When Bethany shows up, desperate for his help, Kirk agrees, ready to resist her seductive charm.

After her breakup with Kirk, Bethany Walker has kept her distance, working hard to move on from her heartache. But Bethany discovers that her estranged father is in danger, and Kirk is the only man she can turn to for help. Seeing Kirk again threatens to reignite the feud between their families, worst of all, endangers her battered heart.

Working together is the toughest challenge either of them has faced. As they uncover the secrets of the past and get closer to the shocking truth, danger lurks around every corner. Will Kirk and Bethany rekindle their relationship or will the war between their families consume them both?

Find Lexy Timms:

LEXY TIMMS NEWSLETTER:
http://eepurl.com/9i0vD
Lexy Timms Facebook Page:
https://www.facebook.com/SavingForever
Lexy Timms Website:
http://www.lexytimms.com

Want

FREE READS?

Sign up for Lexy Timms' newsletter
And she'll send you updates on new releases,
ARC copies of books and a whole lotta fun!
Sign up for news and updates!
http://eepurl.com/9i0vD

More by Lexy Timms:

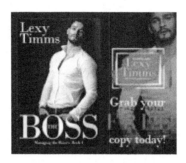

FROM BEST SELLING AUTHOR, Lexy Timms, comes a billionaire romance that'll make you swoon and fall in love all over again.

Jamie Connors has given up on men. Despite being smart, pretty, and just slightly overweight, she's a magnet for the kind of guys that don't stay around.

Her sister's wedding is at the foreground of the family's attention. Jamie would be fine with it if her sister wasn't pressuring her to lose weight so she'll fit in the maid of honor dress, her mother would get off her case and her ex-boyfriend wasn't about to become her brother-in-law.

Determined to step out on her own, she accepts a PA position from billionaire Alex Reid. The job includes an apartment on his property and gets her out of living in her parent's basement.

Jamie has to balance her life and somehow figure out how to manage her billionaire boss, without falling in love with him.

** The Boss is book 1 in the Managing the Bosses series. All your questions won't be answered in the first book. It may end on a cliff hanger.

For mature audiences only. There are adult situations, but this is a love story, NOT erotica.

FRAGILE TOUCH

"HIS BODY IS PERFECT. He's got this face that isn't just heart-melting but actually kind of exotic..."

Lillian Warren's life is just how she's designed it. She has a high-paying job working with celebrities and the elite, teaching them how to better organize their lives. She's on her own, the days quiet, but she likes it that way. Especially since she's still figuring out how to live with her recent diagnosis of Crohn's disease. Her cats keep her company, and she's not the least bit lonely.

Fun-loving personal trainer, Cayden, thinks his neighbor is a killjoy. He's only seen her a few times, and the woman looks like she needs a drink or three. He knows how to party and decides to invite her to over—if he can find her. What better way to impress her than take care of her overgrown yard? She proceeds to thank him by throwing up in his painstakingly-trimmed-to-perfection bushes.

Something about the fragile, mysterious woman captivates him.

Something about this rough-on-the-outside bear of a man attracts Lily, despite her heart warning her to tread carefully.

Faking It Description:

HE GROANED. THIS WAS torture. Being trapped in a room with a beautiful woman was just about every man's fantasy, but he had to remember that this was just pretend.

Allyson Smith has crushed on her boss for years, but never dared to make a move. When she finds herself without a date to her brother's upcoming wedding, Allyson tells her family one innocent white lie: that she's been dating her boss. Unfortunately, her boss discovers her lie, and insists on posing as her boyfriend to escort her to the wedding.

Playboy billionaire Dane Prescott always has a new heiress on his arm, but he can't get his assistant Allyson out of his head. He's fought his attraction to her, until he gets caught up in her scheme of a fake relationship.

One passionate weekend with the boss has Allyson Smith questioning everything she believes in. Falling for a wealthy playboy like Dane is against the rules, but if she's just faking it what's the harm?

Capturing Her Beauty

KAYLA REID HAS ALWAYS been into fashion and everything to do with it. Growing up wasn't easy for her. A bigger girl trying to squeeze into the fashion world is like trying to suck an entire gelatin mold through a straw; possible, but difficult.

She found herself an open door as a designer and jumped right in. Her designs always made the models smile. The colors, the fabrics, the styles. Never once did she dream of being on the other side of the lens. She got to watch her clothing strut around on others and that was good enough.

But who says you can't have a little fun when you're off the clock?

Sometimes trying on the latest fashions is just as good as making them. Kayla's hours in front of the mirror were a guilty pleasure.

A chance meeting with one of the company photographers may turn into more than just an impromptu photo shoot.

Hot n' Handsome, Rich & Single... how far are you willing to go?
MEET ALEX REID, CEO of Reid Enterprise. Billionaire extra ordinaire, chiseled to perfection, panty-melter and currently single.

Learn about Alex Reid before he began Managing the Bosses. Alex Reid sits down for an interview with R&S.

His life style is like his handsome looks: hard, fast, breath-taking and out to play ball. He's risky, charming and determined.

How close to the edge is Alex willing to go? Will he stop at nothing to get what he wants?

Alex Reid is book 1 in the R&S Rich and Single Series. Fall in love with these hot and steamy men; all single, successful, and searching for love.

Book One is FREE!
SOMETIMES THE HEART needs a different kind of saving... find out if Charity Thompson will find a way of saving forever in this hospital setting Best-Selling Romance by Lexy Timms

Charity Thompson wants to save the world, one hospital at a time. Instead of finishing med school to become a doctor, she chooses a different path and raises money for hospitals – new wings, equipment, whatever they need. Except there is one hospital she would be happy to never set foot in again—her fathers. So of course, he hires her to create a gala for his sixty-fifth birthday. Charity can't say no. Now she is working in the one place she doesn't want to be. Except she's attracted to Dr. Elijah Bennet, the handsome playboy chief.

Will she ever prove to her father that's she's more than a med school dropout? Or will her attraction to Elijah keep her from repairing the one thing she desperately wants to fix?

HEART OF THE BATTLE Series

In a world plagued with darkness, she would be his salvation.

No one gave Erik a choice as to whether he would fight or not. Duty to the crown belonged to him, his father's legacy remaining beyond the grave.

Taken by the beauty of the countryside surrounding her, Linzi would do anything to protect her father's land. Britain is under attack and Scotland is next. At a time she should be focused on suitors, the men of her country have gone to war and she's left to stand alone.

Love will become available, but will passion at the touch of the enemy unravel her strong hold first?

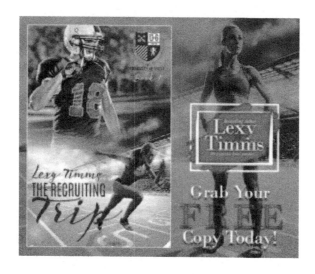

THE RECRUITING TRIP

Aspiring college athlete Aileen Nessa is finding the recruiting process beyond daunting. Being ranked #10 in the world for the 100m hurdles at the age of eighteen is not a fluke, even though she believes that one race, where everything clinked magically together, might be. American universities don't seem to think so. Letters are pouring in from all over the country.

As she faces the challenge of differentiating between a college's genuine commitment to her or just empty promises from talent-seeking coaches, Aileen heads to the University of Gatica, a Division One school, on a recruiting trip. Her best friend dares who to go just to see the cute guys on the school's brochure.

The university's athletic program boasts one of the top hurdlers in the country. Tyler Jensen is the school's NCAA champion in the hurdles and Jim Thorpe recipient for top defensive back in football. His incredible blue-green eyes, confident smile and rock hard six pack abs mess with Aileen's concentration.

His offer to take her under his wing, should she choose to come to Gatica, is a temping proposition that has her wondering if she might be with an angel or making a deal with the devil himself.

THE ONE YOU CAN'T FORGET

Emily Rose Dougherty is a good Catholic girl from mythical Walkerville, CT. She had somehow managed to get herself into a heap trouble with the law, all because an ex-boyfriend has decided to make things difficult.

Luke "Spade" Wade owns a Motorcycle repair shop and is the Road Captain for Hades' Spawn MC. He's shocked when he reads in the paper that his old high school flame has been arrested. She's always been the one he couldn't forget.

Will destiny let them find each other again? Or what happens in the past, best left for the history books?

** *This is book 1 of the Hades' Spawn MC Series. All your questions may not be answered in the first book.*

Did you love *Investing in Love*? Then you should read *Just Me* by Lexy Timms!

We all need somewhere where we feel safe...After leaving her abusive husband, Katherine Marshall is out on her own for the first time. She's hopped from city to city to avoid the man who made her life a living hell. When it seems she's finally found a new place where she begins to feel safe, she slowly grows confident that her life is looking up. A chance meeting with Ben O'Leary sets her life on a course and her soul on fire.Ben launched a business that went on to viral success while he was in college, and now as a thriving entrepreneur, he's most interested in maximizing profits. A billionaire living the dream But all that changes when he sets his eyes on Katherine. Things between the two heat up as they fall hard and fast—that is, until she gets an unexpected surprise that will test the strength of their relationship.You & Me - A Bad Boy RomanceBook 1 – Just MeBook 2 – Touch MeBook 3 – Kiss Me

Read more at www.lexytimms.com.

Also by Lexy Timms

Investing in Love

Billionaire Holiday Romance Series
Driving Home for Christmas
The Valentine Getaway
Cruising Love

Billionaire in Disguise Series
Facade
Illusion
Charade

Billionaire Secrets Series
The Secret
Freedom
Courage
Trust
Impulse
Billionaire Secrets Box Set Books #1-3

Building Billions
Building Billions - Part 1
Building Billions - Part 2
Building Billions - Part 3

For His Pleasure
Elizabeth
Georgia
Madison

Fortune Riders MC Series
Billionaire Biker
Billionaire Ransom
Billionaire Misery

Fragile Series
Fragile Touch
Fragile Kiss
Fragile Love

Hades' Spawn Motorcycle Club
One You Can't Forget
One That Got Away
One That Came Back
One You Never Leave
One Christmas Night
Hades' Spawn MC Complete Series

Hard Rocked Series

Rhyme
Harmony

Heart of Stone Series
The Protector
The Guardian
The Warrior

Heart of the Battle Series
Celtic Viking
Celtic Rune
Celtic Mann
Heart of the Battle Series Box Set

Heistdom Series
Master Thief
Goldmine
Diamond Heist
Smile For Me

Just About Series
About Love
About Truth
About Forever

Justice Series
Seeking Justice
Finding Justice
Chasing Justice
Pursuing Justice
Justice - Complete Series

Love You Series
Love Life
Need Love
My Love

Managing the Bosses Series
The Boss
The Boss Too
Who's the Boss Now
Love the Boss
I Do the Boss
Wife to the Boss
Employed by the Boss
Brother to the Boss
Senior Advisor to the Boss
Forever the Boss
Christmas With the Boss
Gift for the Boss - Novella 3.5

Model Mayhem Series
Shameless
Modesty
Imperfection

Moment in Time
Highlander's Bride
Victorian Bride
Modern Day Bride
A Royal Bride
Forever the Bride

Outside the Octagon
Submit

Protecting Diana Series
Her Bodyguard
Her Defender
Her Champion
Her Protector
Her Forever

Protecting Layla Series
His Mission

Reverse Harem Series
Primals
Archaic
Unitary

RIP Series
Track the Ripper
Hunt the Ripper
Pursue the Ripper

R&S Rich and Single Series
Alex Reid
Parker

Saving Forever
Saving Forever - Part 1
Saving Forever - Part 2
Saving Forever - Part 3
Saving Forever - Part 4
Saving Forever - Part 5
Saving Forever - Part 6
Saving Forever Part 7
Saving Forever - Part 8
Saving Forever Boxset Books #1-3

Shifting Desires Series
Jungle Heat
Jungle Fever
Jungle Blaze

Southern Romance Series
Little Love Affair
Siege of the Heart
Freedom Forever
Soldier's Fortune

Tattooist Series
Confession of a Tattooist
Surrender of a Tattooist
Heart of a Tattooist
Hopes & Dreams of a Tattooist

Tennessee Romance
Whisky Lullaby
Whisky Melody
Whisky Harmony

The Bad Boy Alpha Club
Battle Lines - Part 1

Battle Lines

The Brush Of Love Series
Every Night
Every Day
Every Time
Every Way
Every Touch

The Debt
The Debt: Part 1 - Damn Horse
The Debt: Complete Collection

The University of Gatica Series
The Recruiting Trip
Faster
Higher
Stronger
Dominate
No Rush
University of Gatica - The Complete Series

T.N.T. Series
Troubled Nate Thomas - Part 1
Troubled Nate Thomas - Part 2
Troubled Nate Thomas - Part 3

Undercover Series
Perfect For Me
Perfect For You
Perfect For Us

Unknown Identity Series
Unknown
Unpublished
Unexposed
Unsure
Unwritten
Unknown Identity Box Set: Books #1-3

Unlucky Series
Unlucky in Love
UnWanted
UnLoved Forever

Wet & Wild Series
Stormy Love
Savage Love
Secure Love

Worth It Series

Worth Billions
Worth Every Cent
Worth More Than Money

You & Me - A Bad Boy Romance
Just Me
Touch Me

Standalone
Wash
Loving Charity
Summer Lovin'
Love & College
Billionaire Heart
First Love
Frisky and Fun Romance Box Collection
Managing the Bosses Box Set #1-3

Watch for more at www.lexytimms.com.

About the Author

"Love should be something that lasts forever, not is lost forever."

Visit USA TODAY BESTSELLING AUTHOR, LEXY TIMMS
https://www.facebook.com/SavingForever

Please feel free to connect with me and share your comments. I love connecting with my readers.

Sign up for news and updates and freebies - I like spoiling my readers!

http://eepurl.com/9i0vD

website: www.lexytimms.com

Dealing in Antique Jewelry and hanging out with her awesome hubby and three kids, Lexy Timms loves writing in her free time.

MANAGING THE BOSSES is a bestselling 10-part series dipping into the lives of Alex Reid and Jamie Connors. Can a secretary really fall for her billionaire boss?

Read more at www.lexytimms.com.

Made in the USA
Coppell, TX
26 December 2020